Also by Kjartan Poskitt

Urgum the Axeman
Urgum and the Seat of Flames

The *Murderous Maths* series
Isaac Newton and his Apple
The Gobsmacking Galaxy
A Brief History of Pants
The Magic of Pants

URGUM

AND THE

GOO GOO BAH!

Kjartan Poskitt illustrated by Philip Reeve

■SCHOLASTIC

First published in the UK in 2008 by Scholastic Children's Books
An imprint of Scholastic Ltd
Euston House, 24 Eversholt Street
London, NW1 1DB, UK
Registered office: Westfield Road, Southam, Warwickshire, CV47 0RA
SCHOLASTIC and associated logos are trademarks and/or registered
trademarks of Scholastic Inc.

Text copyright © Kjartan Poskitt, 2008
Cover and inside illustrations © Philip Reeve, 2008
The rights of Kjartan Poskitt and Philip Reeve to be identified as the
author and illustrator of this work have been asserted by them.

ISBN 978 1 407 10811 7

Printed by CPI Bookmarque. Croydon, CR0 4TD
Papers used by Scholastic Children's Books are
made from wood grown in sustainable forests.

3 5 7 9 10 8 6 4 2

This is a work of fiction. Names, characters, places, incidents and dialogues are
products of the author's imagination or are used fictitiously. Any resemblance
to actual people, living or dead, events or locales is entirely coincidental.

www.scholastic.co.uk/zone

*For Bridget and
our four Mollys*

CONTENTS

PROLOGUE

PART ONE

THE OUTCAST

PART ONE AND A HALF

A DATE IS MADE

PART TWO

THE RATTLE BATTLE

PART THREE

THE UNINTERESTING TUNNELS

Molly

Ruff

Divina

Ruinn

Urgum
the
Axe Man

The
Other
One →

Rakk and
Rekk

Raymond

Robbin

The Prologue:
Disappearing Footsteps

The hairy hands reached out of the darkness into the cradle but once again they found it empty. There was a soft growl of frustration, then the hands groped their way over to the foot of the magnificent bed. Very carefully they felt their way up to the top of the silken quilt where two sleeping heads were gently breathing side by side. The rough fingers tried to ease the quilt back but they got entangled in something long, wispy and completely nexpected. The larger head stirred and

1

groaned, the hands tugged themselves free.

"GUARDS!"

Footsteps scuttled away across the tiled floor, there was a creak of hinges and a dull thud as a trapdoor fell shut. While keys rattled outside, the princess leapt from her bed, scooped up the baby and ran to face the wall. No one, not even her closest staff, was ever allowed to lay eyes on her accursed beauty. The door burst open and the room was filled with clunking boots and the glint of swords in candlelight.

"There's no one here, your majesty," came a concerned woman's voice.

"Somebody *was* here."

"But the door was locked and there are no windows," insisted a pompous man's voice. "Perhaps her majesty was having another of her dreams."

"These are NOT dreams! Thake, dismiss your guards and go. But Jannilah, please, you stay."

The boots clunked off down the corridor, but it wasn't until she heard the door close that the princess turned away from the wall and came back to the bed. She gently settled her baby on a pillow, then looked up at her Mistress of the Royal Bedchamber, who was holding a candlestick. Jannilah was dressed in her immaculate white robes, and as ever there was a thick band wrapped safely across her eyes.

"Oh Jannilah, you believe me, don't you? He'll never be safe until this threat is over."

The mistress nodded her head. "I do believe your majesty. And don't despair. I also believe I have the answer."

PART ONE

THE Outcast

A Spot of Rain

"Hey, come and get me! Oy! Robbin? Ruff? ANYONE? I'm drowning out here! Can't you count, any of you? PLEASE! I mean it!"

But the voice from the little old leather bag lying in the middle of Golgarth Basin could hardly be heard among the howls of thunder and the screech of the rain. It didn't rain often in the Lost Desert, but when it did, it rained in style. Huge boulders that had been baking for months under the white-hot sun were hissing under the deluge and filling the rock basin with a heavy swirling fog. Large bubbling puddles quickly spread and merged into a thrashing lake, which rose up around the bag, making it lurch over and drift about aimlessly.

"Hello?" shouted the voice from the bag. "Anyone there? Anyone? Oh, forget it." The voice took a deep breath and then puffed out of the open end of the bag. Slowly the bag steered itself around, and then, as the puffing continued, made its way purposefully across the basin towards a cave at the far side.

Strung across the entrance to the cave was a heavy leather curtain which was being held aside by the fiercest savage that the Lost Desert had ever known. His weather-whipped face grinned excitedly, showing off his sharpened teeth.

"I love storms," said Urgum the Axeman, leaning on the handle of his double-headed axe and gazing at the chaos outside. "Just look at it. Jags of lightning, whacks of thunder, a screaming wind – it's true barbarian weather, isn't it, boys?"

"Yeah!" came a cheer from behind him. Urgum's seven savage sons were tough, hard and brutal, so they really loved storms too, but they weren't watching because with the curtain open it was just a bit on the chilly side. Instead the tough, hard, brutal sons were huddled round the fire picking their toes and hoping something warm to eat would turn up soon without them having to do anything.

Standing next to Urgum was a woman who looked like she couldn't possibly be his wife, but she was. Divina was an elegant softhand, he was a filthy savage. Her face and hands were scrubbed clean, his hands were filthy and savage. Her old blue dress had been carefully washed and pressed, his trousers were filthy and savage. She could count up to nine hundred and seventeen. He could only count to one, and even that one was a pretty filthy and savage one too. You couldn't get two people who were more different.

"I've never seen such a storm," said Divina.

"It's a belter, isn't it?" chuckled Urgum. "If one blast of that lightning hit you, POW, you'd turn into a kebab."

"I hope none of the boys are out there," said Divina. She called back to the group round the fire. "Are you lot all here?"

"Yeah, yeah, yeah," muttered the boys boredly. Why did mums always make such a fuss about stupid things like having their sons turned into kebabs?

"Just count yourselves to make sure," she insisted.

Back in the flickery orange gloom of the cave, the boys all stared round at each other and shrugged their shoulders. It was best to do what their mother said.

"One," said Ruff, the eldest, pointing at himself.

"One," said Ruinn, the skinny weird one, also pointing at himself.

"One," said Robbin, the biggest.

"Hang on!" said Divina. "What do you mean one … one … one? There's supposed to be seven of you."

"You said count ourselves," said Ruff. "Well, there's only one of me. So that's one."

"And there's only one of me," said all the others.

Urgum chuckled at his wife. "All this fancy mathematical counting, that's just for softhands. ONE is all you need. Other numbers are just lots of ones put together, isn't that right, boys?"

"Yeah!"

Divina bit her lip and stared out at the patterns in the

swirling fog. Sometimes the limits of the barbarian brain made her want to scream, but screaming wasn't Divina's style. Her style was to get her own back, and she knew the perfect way to do it.

"Do you think this storm is a divine sign from your gods?" she asked unscreamingly.

"Wow! Yes, of course, it must be!" Urgum looked up at the rumbling skies in delight. "Lightning, thunder, mayhem, chaos … it's weather served up barbarian style. But what are they trying to say?"

"It's obvious. Your gods want us to wash your trousers."

"WASH MY TROUSERS?"

gasped Urgum.

"I can't think of anything else that would need so much water," said Divina, looking at the lake that stretched right across Golgarth Basin.

"NOBODY is washing my trousers. Washing my trousers is punishable by

DEATH."

"Now, now, dear, you've had them on for years, so don't argue with your gods."

"I'm not arguing with my gods," cursed Urgum. "I'm arguing with you! All my gods want me to do is to continue the honoured barbarian tradition of fighting and dying gloriously and gruesomely. Trouser washing doesn't come into it."

"So why did they send so much water down, then?"

"Because, well, because…"

Just then a girl's head squeezed between them. "Hi, Dad! Is this a private argument or can anybody join in?"

"Of course you can join in, Molly," said Urgum. "So long as you're on the right side."

"Which side is furthest away from your smelly trousers?" asked Molly.

"Don't you start!" moaned Urgum. "I'll ask the gods what they mean myself." Urgum stuck his head out of the cave entrance and looked up to the skies.

"TANGOR! TANGAL!"

he cried. "It is I, Urgum, your champion. I demand to know, have you sent this storm to make me wash my trousers? Well?"

Urgum's voice carried far and away up above the skies to the Hallowed Halls of Sirrus, where the twin barbarian gods had been having an after-dinner snooze. Tangor was sprawled back in his mighty seat of marble, completely oblivious to the fact that his thunderous snoring, electrostatic rumblings and torrential dribbling had been causing arguments down at Golgarth Cragg. On hearing Urgum's shout, his twin sister, Tangal, had stirred and given him a prod.

"Tangor," she said. "Listen! Urgum's shouting something at us."

"Eh, what … who?" burbled Tangor, still half-asleep.

"Urgum!" said Tangal. "Our last true barbarian champion. He's shouting but I can't hear him. Shut up and listen."

So Tangor shut up and listened.

Down below, a final bolt of lightning hit the top of the cragg wall and smashed a boulder into sand.

GAKKA-BOSHHHH

The particles hissed down on to the water and then everything went quiet. The storm had stopped dead, just like that.

Urgum wasn't pleased. "Happy now?" he sulked, letting the leather curtain drop across the entrance. "Because I'm not. You two are an embarrassment. That was an awesome show my gods were putting on, but you had to go and spoil it by talking about washing trousers."

"Hang on, Dad, there's something out there," said Molly, pulling back the curtain again. The surface of the water was lying flat, like a giant mirror. The only disturbance was a set of small ripples coming from a lumpy brown something twitching away in the middle. It seemed to be making slow and painful progress towards them. "It's one of Raymond's bags!"

"Raymond?" said Urgum. "What's he doing out there?"

It was a tricky question. In fact, it was tricky to tell what Raymond was doing *anywhere*. That's because, years ago, Urgum's cleverest son had stumbled into a pit of razor snakes which had sliced him into forty-seven separate pieces. Luckily for him, the gods had kept him alive, but unluckily for him, he'd been living in a

selection of bags ever since.

"My baby!" squealed Divina. "But I counted all his bags, they're stacked up in the corner."

"Ha ha!" scoffed Urgum. Now it was his chance to get his own back on Divina. "That shows you how useless counting is. I tell you, as soon as you try to count past one, there's problems."

Molly wasn't so sure. Divina was the best counter in the cave, and if she said Raymond's bags were all there, then something strange must have happened. Raymond wouldn't sneak one of his bags out without telling anyone. He just wasn't the type. Meanwhile, Divina was quietly hissing, because once again Urgum was looking far too pleased with himself.

"Well?" said Divina.

"Well what?" said Urgum.

"Are you going to get him?"

"Don't look at me," said Urgum. "I'm not the one who pretends I can count bags of body bits."

"Urgum, that's your son out there!"

"It's not all of him, it's only one bit," said Urgum. "Anyway, he's the one in trouble, not me. He should have learnt to swim."

"And can you swim?"

"That's not important."

"But can you?"

"Barbarians don't do water! Water is a softhand washy thing."

"It's not that deep, Dad," said Molly. "You could just paddle over, so you needn't be scared."

"Scared? ME? Barbarians are scared of nothing."

"Then why don't you just paddle out there and get him?" said Divina.

"Why don't YOU paddle out there and get him?"

Even before the words had come out of his mouth, Urgum was regretting them. Divina turned to face him full on with her arms folded tightly and her mouth set hard. She was all ready to bring her most dangerous weapon into play. Eeeek! Slowly she raised her left eyebrow. Urgum shivered. What was it about that eyebrow that could plant panic in parts that nothing else could touch? Urgum had chewed the tail off a unicorn, he'd single-handedly defeated the Fat Mutts of Nugg, he'd even worn the Flaming Pants of Shumbitt, but none of them had quite turned his guts in the way that eyebrow could. Somehow it had the power to make him feel useless, pathetic and ashamed.

"In case you hadn't realized," said Divina, ice-cold and

deathly calm, "I have just combed my HAIR."

Urgum blinked and shook his head, trying to work out what combed hair had to do with not paddling. He studied Divina carefully, and sure enough, her dark hair was neatly piled up on the top end of her body, and her feet were still down at the bottom end. Paddling/hair – no, he couldn't see the connection at all. In desperation, he turned to Molly.

"She says she's combed her hair," he said weakly, hoping for a bit of support or guidance or even just a few words that made sense to him.

"She has, Dad, honest," nodded Molly. "So you'll have to go."

There wasn't a weapon built or a monster born that could defeat Urgum the Axeman, but when Divina's eyebrow was coupled up to a bit of heartless female logic…

Splosh Splosh Splosh

As Urgum gingerly set out from the cave, Molly watched his huge shoulders shudder as he tried to cope with the unfamiliar feeling of water seeping between his toes.

"Mum," said Molly (slightly confused). "How come he's the fiercest savage that the Lost Desert has ever known, but he does what you say?"

"Because he's gorgeous."

"Mum," said Molly (even more confused). "How is he gorgeous when his trousers are so smelly?"

"His gorgeousness overshadows the smelliness of his trousers."

"Mum," said Molly (desperately confused). "If he's so full of gorgeousnessness, why do you make him do something he hates?"

"Because he thinks it's clever that he can only count to ONE," said Divina. "And that, my dear Molly, is how it works."

"Ah, I see," said Molly (100 per cent confused).

The Reluctant Lifeguard

The silvery sheet of water stretched as far as Urgum could see through the thinning fog. Some anxious ostriches had gathered in a sheltered corner by the cragg wall and were looking down at their own reflections. They were wondering why their legs were twice as long as normal and why they each had another ostrich on the other end looking back up at them.

Urgum paddled out towards the bag and had to admire how a bit of water could make everything look so different. There was no sign of the well-worn tracks leading to all the other places, such as the watchtower, the horse rails and the other caves. It was even hard to tell which was the lynching tree because the old bone pile underneath it was submerged.

"Hey, Urgum!" A deep voice boomed out from the other side of the basin. It was Urgum's oldest, ugliest and bestest friend, Mungoid the Ungoid, looking out of his cave. He'd been happily crunching away at a bison's rib bone when he'd seen Urgum gingerly picking his way through the water. "What are you doing with wet feet?"

Urgum stuck his thumb over his shoulder to point back at his cave and shrugged his shoulders helplessly.

"Oh, the eyebrow again," muttered Mungoid to himself. He nodded in sympathy. He didn't have a wife or anybody else living in his cave with him. Sometimes it was a bit lonely, but at least he didn't have an eyebrow telling him what to do. Poor old Urgum, but thankfully the bag was almost within his reach. Suddenly Mungoid had a nasty thought.

"Urgum, STOP!"

Urgum froze and looked around uncertainly.

"The bear pit!" shouted Mungoid. "It must be around there somewhere."

Urgum had forgotten about the steep hole in the ground where they used to keep wild bears. It would be full of water, but where was it? The water was unusually shiny (because it had dribbled down from the snoring god), so even when Urgum looked down at his feet, all he could see was his face, peering over his tubby tum, looking back up at him. He was just about to ask Mungoid where he thought the pit might be when the cave door next to Mungoid's opened. The great Ungoid watched excitedly as a tall female savage in tight skirmish armour stepped out. Clearly she hadn't expected to see the flooded basin and had no intention of wading through it, but before she could go back in, Mungoid dared himself to try out the cool new chat-up line he'd been working on.

"Good morning, Grizelda," he said, smoothing down the three hairs that stuck out of the top of his head. "By the way, your elbows smell very nice."

Grizelda the

Grizly gave him a curious look, and although she didn't smile, she didn't not smile either. With a swirl of her fabulous flame-coloured hair, she disappeared back inside.

TWINK
PLINK
DINK

Mungoid's three hairs shot back up. Urgum knew that Mungoid would already be far too busy inventing an even cooler chat-up line to be bothered with bear pits now, but just ahead of him was the bag, and the water only came halfway up the side. It could only be ankle-deep, so at least Urgum knew that the bear pit couldn't be there. Just to make extra sure, Urgum stamped his feet to check that the ground was solid. The sploshing of the water sent out ripples which pushed the bag back a bit.

"Do you mind?" The voice in the bag sounded puffed out. "I was just starting to make a bit of progress."

"Oh, that's very nice, I must say," said Urgum. "Especially as I've come to rescue you."

"And about time too. What kept you, you lazy lump?"

"Look, matey," said Urgum crossly. "I've had to wade through solid water to get here, so if you want rescuing, you better change your attitude."

"Oh go on then. You may as well take me back now you're here."

"*May as well?* You'll have to ask nicer than that. You have to say pretty please."

"Pretty please oh lovely super Daddy, please please take me back to the cave so I can get dried out PLEASE. There, happy now?"

No, Urgum wasn't happy, but he knew Divina would make him even unhappier if he got back to the cave without Raymond's bag.

"People shouldn't need rescuing, it's pathetic," said Urgum, taking one last step forward.

SLAPPA-BLOOSH!

Urgum disappeared. The leather bag was sploshed and rocked around as he tried to scrabble out of the submerged bear pit. First his foot stuck out of the water, then his bottom, and finally a hand appeared frantically grasping for anything it could reach. The fingers closed around a loose strap on the bag.

"Careful!" shouted Raymond's voice.

Urgum heaved on the strap and managed to right himself so that his head broke through the surface, snorting and guffing water.

"What happened to the ground?" he belched.

"There isn't any ground here!" said the voice from the bag. "I'm floating, or at least I'm trying to. Let go."

"No!" wailed Urgum, grabbing on with both hands. "Get me to the side."

"Oh," said the voice. "So you want rescuing, do you? Isn't that a bit pathetic?"

"I ORDER you," shouted Urgum.

"That's no good. You have to ask nicely. Say pretty please."

"Grrrr," said Urgum.

"Tum te tum," said the bag. "I'm waiting…"

The Little Guest

Urgum's other sons had joined Molly and Divina in the cave entrance to watch the fun, but luckily for Urgum they were too far away to make out exactly what was happening. Although it seemed like Urgum was pushing Raymond's bag along, in truth the bag was puffing away with all its might, and terribly terribly slowly it was dragging Urgum across the sunken bear pit.

"Dad's so brave," said Molly. "I can't believe he dived in to save Raymond when he hates water and can't swim."

"It'll be ages before he gets back at that rate," said Ruff. "And I'm hungry."

"I still don't understand what the bag was doing

there," said Divina, trying to think back. Before the rains came, they had all been sitting outside the entrance to Golgarth Cragg, and Raymond's bags had been piled on the rocks. As soon as the first thunder broke, the boys had grabbed the bags and run inside, where Divina had counted them. How had one got left out?

Divina went to the back of the cave and counted again. There were thirteen bags, all twitching with Raymond's various body bits, exactly as it should be, and yet there was Urgum with another bag out in the water. Just as she was pondering this, a little whimpery noise came from one of the bags! The other bags full of Raymond's living body parts, all rolled and scuppered away, leaving a slightly newer bag sitting on its own.

"What is it, Mum?" asked Molly.

Cautiously they opened the bag and peered in. A pair of dark eyes peered out.

goo goo
bah

"A baby!" gasped Molly. "Somebody must have left it with the other bags."

"And when we were dashing in we didn't notice the wrong bag," said Divina.

goo goo bah

Divina opened the bag further to see a very little person in a tidy grey smock and soft brown woolly socks. The baby was clean and looked healthy, obviously it had been cared for. The little face stared back up at them, then a little fist found its way into its mouth.

wah wah... ummm

"It's sucking its fist," said Molly.

"It'll be hungry," said Divina. "There's some milk and a bit of bread in the kitchen, I'll get it."

Divina disappeared through the dark arch at the back of the cave leaving Molly cradling the baby on her knee. Gradually the boys turned their attention away from the fire to find the dark eyes staring at them.

goo goo bah

"What's that then?" demanded Ruff the eldest.

"It's a baby boy," said Molly. "It was in a bag."

"Best place for it," said Ruff. "Anyway, how do you know it's a boy? You've had a look, haven't you?"

"I didn't need to look," said Molly. She lifted the baby up so its bottom was next to her nose and pretended to sniff. "You're a boy and it smells like you."

"Ha ha ha!" went all the others.

goo goo bah

Molly got up and carried the baby over to the fire.

"Let me introduce my lovely brothers," she said. "First there's Robbin."

The biggest son got to his feet and reached out a massive hand so that its tiny fist could wrap around his fingertip. Very solemnly they shook hands.

"Hello little friend," he said. "What's your name?"

goo goo bah

"Googoobah?" exclaimed Robbin. "That's a well-cool name for a savage."

The little face broke into a huge smile.

"A savage?" said the twins. Rekk and Rakk leapt up to their feet and pushed in front of their large brother.

"That little thing doesn't look very savage," said Rakk.

"This is what savage looks like!" said Rekk, pulling a scary savage face and doing a savage **GRRR** noise.

"Call that savage?" scoffed Rakk. "*This* is savage." And he pulled an even savager face and did an even **GRRRRIER GRRRR** noise.

They both stood there pulling their faces and *grrr*ing and waiting for the baby to cry. But the baby just stuck out his tongue and did a little dribbly raspberry. The twins turned on each other.

"Were you supposed to be looking savage?"

"I was savager than you."

"Rubbish, you couldn't even scare a baby!"

"Yes I could. You're a baby and you're scared of me."

"Scared? Of you? Me?" said Rekk, who then realized that he'd run out of clever things to say, so instead he punched his brother in the jaw with a big

SMUNCH.

"Ooof!" said Rakk, who then discovered that he'd run out of clever things to say too, so he replied with a mighty

WAMBiFFSHMOCK BLATTERKLUMP.

Needless to say, two savage twins brutally punching, biting and ripping bits off each other was fine entertainment for babies.

google google goo

he laughed delightedly.

"Stop it!" shouted Molly, hugging the googling baby to her chest. "You're getting him too excited. He'll be ill!"

A tall eerie figure stood up, the orange firelight glimmering on his long pointed teeth. "I'll stop him laughing," said Ruinn nastily. The skinny son shoved his long bony nose into the baby's face and leered his ghastliest leer, the one that he used to make rattlesnakes bite their own tails off. Molly had seen Ruinn's leer before, but it was still enough to make her feel a bit shaky until she remembered that it was only Ruinn and he had a spotty bottom. As for the baby, his little lower lip quivered but he wasn't ready to burst into tears yet. Two little hands shot out and grabbed Ruinn's eyelids and twisted them, digging the tiny fingernails in.

"Yee-OWWW!"

screamed Ruinn.

"Wow!" gasped the others in admiration, then they broke into a chant.

"GO BABY! GO BABY! GO BABY!"

Ruinn managed to pull himself away and staggered back against the wall.

"Serves you right for trying to be scary," grinned Molly. "Now, who else is there?"

A hand stuck out of one of Raymond's bags and waved and the baby waved back. Then another son stood up and waved and said hello and mentioned something or other but nobody ever bothered about him. Instead Molly took the baby over to see Ruff, who was sitting on the floor, knees drawn up to his chest, staring into the fire.

"Take that thing away," said Ruff.

"Aw!" said Molly. "You're just jealous because he's getting all the attention, aren't you?"

"I AM the oldest," said Ruff. "And I don't remember anybody asking ME if I wanted a baby in here."

"So?" said Molly.

Ruff got to his feet, turned to face them and crossed his arms bossily.

"So I say it goes," said Ruff. "What have you got to say

to that, squitty?"

The baby didn't exactly say anything, but the message was clear enough. His mouth opened wide and…

BURR-LOOOSH

…a beautifully detonated burp shot out a thick stream of white vomit, which hit Ruff in the teeth and splattered all over his head. Even Ruinn stopped feeling sorry for himself and joined in the applause.

"GO BABY! GO BABY! GO BABY!"

Divina came back in with a small bowl of white mushy stuff.

"Watch out, Ruff," laughed Ruinn. "We're going to reload him."

Soon the baby was reloaded and then put back into his bag for a nap. It was just in time too, because a few sharp POP noises were coming from the kitchen. A fat rhino had been roasting over the fire for a few days and its toenails had just exploded, which meant it was ready. (You have to be careful not to overroast rhino, otherwise it melts into something like stringy strawberry jelly.)

Robbin helped Divina and Molly chop half of it into buckets to eat immediately, but they were careful to leave the rest for Urgum. They knew when he got back he'd be barbarically cross, and the only thing that would calm him down was a completely ridiculous amount of food.

Sure enough, when Urgum eventually squelched into the cave and dumped Raymond's wet bag by the fire, he was so furious that his ears were smoking. He was cross that he was wet and he was double cross that his trousers were very slightly cleaner than they had been, but his crossest bit of crossness was because he'd been forced to say pretty please to a talking bag. Barbarians simply don't say pretty please, so to make up for it he would have to do something very barbaric and very savage. But what? Whatever it was, it would have to wait until after lunch. He was starving.

The boys scattered to the edges of the cave, leaving Urgum to stand and steam away by the fire. Divina was holding the bag with the baby, but she knew she'd better not mention it until Urgum had had an awful lot to eat.

"Well done, Urgie," said Divina cautiously. "Now let me get you an awful lot to eat."

The cooking smell was so fantastic that Urgum's big nose had been dancing round his face in excitement, but suddenly it had got suspicious.

SNiFF
SNiFFiTY
SNiFF
SNiFFFFF

... there was something wrong.

"What am I getting?" asked Urgum.

"Half a roasted rhino," said Divina.

"HALF?" shouted Urgum's mouth, while his nose did a triumphant snorty sniff. "I knew it! There wasn't enough smell for a whole one. What about the other half?"

"It was yum!" said Ruinn.

"YUM!" agreed the others.

"Oh," said Urgum. "So you've had yours, have you?

Didn't wait for me, did you?"

"There, there, dear," said Divina. "There's plenty left, and you deserve it after all that swimming."

A low chuckle came from Raymond's voice bag. "Swimming? Him?"

With an angry curse, Urgum grabbed the bag and held it over the hottest bit of the fire. The flames licked around the leather, making black scorch marks appear.

"Ooh ow! Put me back!" screamed the bag, so Urgum chucked it back on the ground again. He promised himself he'd definitely do something very barbaric and very savage later, but first it was lunchtime.

KERR-UMPCH

A big crash came from the kitchen.

"What was that?" gasped Molly.

"Oh dear," said Divina, and the two of them dashed through, leaving Urgum pacing around crossly and snarling. The boys shuddered in fear, hoping the noise had just been an egg rolling off the table. But the egg would have needed to be the size of a horse and the table as high as a tree.

"That's very odd," said Urgum. "It sounded like half a roasted rhino falling down a mysterious hole that's suddenly appeared in the kitchen floor."

"Ha ha ha!" laughed the boys nervously. "Good one, Dad."

In the kitchen, Divina and Molly were standing on the

edge of a deep black hole where the rhino had been roasting. In the darkness far below, they could just about make out a few last glowing embers of the fire.

"All this rainwater!" gasped Divina. "It's soaked under the kitchen floor and washed the ground away and taken your father's lunch with it."

Back in the main part of the cave, the boys were still laughing at Urgum's great joke about the mysterious hole.

"Ha ha ha ha ha … erk!"

They had just seen the horrified expression on Divina's face as she came back. The boys all backed up against the wall in panic.

"I KNEW IT!" said Urgum. "You wasters have all been sitting round doing nothing apart from eating, and now I'm left with NO LUNCH. Well, I'm starving, and that reminds me of an old barbarian tradition. Do you know what barbarian tribes used to do when there wasn't enough food for everybody?"

"What was that?" nobody asked. Well, there wasn't much point, obviously he was going to tell them anyway.

"The weakest boy would be cast out."

"Why?" nobody asked again.

"That made one less mouth to feed. Then the strongest can go on and survive."

The boys glanced at each other, then pointed at Molly.

"Why can't it be a girl?" demanded Ruinn.

"Yeah, Dad, why can't I be cast out? That's unfair," said Molly.

"Because tribes need women to … er … well, make more boys so we can cast the weakest out," said Urgum. "You see? These old traditions all make sense. That's why if you call yourselves barbarians, you should stick to them."

Urgum had only meant to give them a fright, but to his surprise, the eldest son, Ruff, got to his feet. There was a nasty smile on his face. "I agree!" he said. "Our father has not eaten. Therefore the weakest boy must suffer."

The other boys all gasped in horror. What was Ruff

saying? With Urgum in this mood he didn't need encouraging to do something ghastly. Each boy desperately hoped for two things. Please let the ghastly thing be done to one of the others. And please let me watch.

"Well, Father?" insisted Ruff. "You claim to be the last of the true barbarians, don't you?"

Urgum nodded solemnly. It wasn't often he agreed with his pompous number one son, but this time Ruff was dead right. Urgum had devoted his entire life to mindless savagery, brutal greed and whiffy trousers. There would never be a truer barbarian than him.

"And so it's up to you to uphold the barbarian traditions," said Ruff.

Urgum couldn't quite see where this was going, but he felt he had to say something suitable for the occasion.

"YARGHHHH!" he said suitably.

"And you didn't get any lunch, did you?"

"NOOOOOOO!" said Urgum.

"Then you must take the weakest boy out to Sacrifice Rock and leave him there for the fates to take their course," said Ruff.

"YARGHHHH!" agreed Urgum.

"But who's the weakest?" said Robbin.

"He is!" Rekk and Rakk jabbed their fingers at each other, then shouted, "No, not me. YOU!"

"Nah," said Ruinn. "It's got to be Raymond. He's all chopped up into bits. That makes you pretty weak."

The others all turned their attention to the pile of bags in the corner. "Yeah, it's Raymond!" they cried. "Cast out Raymond, cast out Raymond."

Urgum heard a voice scowling down by his feet. Raymond's voice bag was still drying out by the fire next to where Urgum was standing. "Don't even think about it, Dad," said Raymond. "Or I'll tell them what you said to me when you were in the water. Remember? Two little words…"

Urgum gulped. NOBODY must ever know he'd said pretty please. But now that Ruff had insisted on the tradition being carried out, SOMEBODY had to suffer. But who?

The boys were arguing again but Ruff raised his hand for silence. To his amazement, he got it.

"I am the eldest son," he said pompously. "And therefore it falls to me to declare the weakest boy."

"It's you!" the others all shouted.

"Oh no, not me," announced Ruff with great evil smugness. He was pointing at the bag that Divina was still cradling. "It's the baby."

All the wet, hungry, furious thoughts that had been screaming through Urgum's brain suddenly went blank.

"Baby?" he said.

The Long Walk

The overhead sun was so white that it was blue, and already the ground in the basin was fizzing and steaming as the last of the rainwater boiled away. Urgum still wasn't quite sure how he'd ended up walking towards the crack in the cragg wall carrying the baby in the bag. He tried to think over what had happened. Wet trousers – no dinner – very cross – barbarian tradition – weakest boy – Sacrifice Rock … it all seemed to follow on. Even though Ruff was a pompous irritating whingey little snot, he'd been right. If food was going to disappear down holes in the ground, they really didn't need another mouth to feed.

But what had surprised Urgum most had been Divina's reaction. Divina had been brought up as a softhand, and if anybody was going to get gooey about abandoning a baby on a rock in the middle of the desert, surely it would have been her. Molly had certainly made her feelings clear, screaming, shouting and threatening never to talk to anybody ever again. And although the boys had been chanting "outcast outcast", they hadn't really been enjoying it as much as good savages should. Ruff had just stood there grinning and picking some strange white goo out of his ear, but why had Divina just handed the bag over without so much as an eyebrow twitch? Even when Molly had threatened to set fire to her mother's hair, Divina had just said, "Your father must do the right thing." *Oooh-er*, thought Urgum. It was all a bit queer.

At first Urgum slung the bag with the baby across his shoulder as if he was just lugging a sack of cannonballs to the watchtower. What did he care if he had to leave a tiny helpless baby out on Sacrifice Rock? He was a tough merciless savage. He was always doing tough merciless things like that, but feeling the warm lump bouncing against his back didn't seem right, especially as it kept saying goo goo bah. Urgum swung the bag down and carried it by his side like a shopping bag.

goo goo bah

He tried swinging the bag a bit, maybe the baby would rock to sleep.

goo goo bah

No, that was no good either. By the time he got to the crack in the wall, he was gently cradling the bag in both arms and peering in at the eyes that stared back at him.

"You'll be all right," said Urgum. "Being cast out's not so bad. Either someone will find you, or, well … soon you'll go up to join the gods. That'll be fun! Hey, you could join my gods. I'm the last of the true barbarians, you know, and my gods are brilliant. They'll be listening to me talking to you now, so don't you worry, they'll be expecting you. Little babies have got nothing to fear from barbarians. We like fighting big tough horrible people, not babies. We look after babies so that they can grow up into big tough horrible people for us to fight and kill."

Urgum was still talking to the bag as he passed under a very long, very sharp and very nasty blood-spattered metal blade. As ever, Olk the giant guardian of Golgarth was standing on duty in the crack in the wall, with his fearsome sword poised over his shoulder. Rumour had it that Olk once sliced an elephant in half with one swipe. Maybe he did, maybe he didn't, but the only way in and out of the basin was past Olk, and scattered around on the nearby rocks were the bones of people who had tried to get in without the password.

"This is Olk," said Urgum to the bag. "He's my friend, you'll like him."

The dark eyes peered out of the bag at the huge head towering over Urgum.

goo goo bah

Olk stood motionless. Urgum brought the bag up close to his face and whispered into it.

"Olk can't talk to you right now," he confided. "He's busy guarding. Anyway, I'm just going to check I've got the right password so that he lets us back in. Sorry, I mean so that he lets *me* back in. Not you, of course."

Urgum suddenly felt a bit stupid, so to try and make himself feel better he took a deep breath and put on a jolly smile. "Well, Olk, old buddy, I'd better be getting on. Things to do and all that. Just checking the password – cheese knife?"

Very slowly the huge head moved down and then back up.

"Right then! Wave goodbye to your uncle Olk, baby." Urgum set off, trying to remember the best way to Sacrifice Rock, and didn't notice a tiny hand stick out from the bag and do a little wave. In return, the massive fingers wrapped around Olk's sword handle did a little flutter. The giant guardian of Golgarth had waved back.

* * *

Urgum headed off down the track that led away from the cragg. A row of stakes had been driven into the ground on either side, and for decoration each one had a skull on the top. To some people, skulls all look pretty much the same, but to Urgum each one of them grinned at him in a slightly different way. He loved how they seemed to pay him their respects as he passed, it always cheered him up, and that's why it was called Smiley Alley.

Urgum had just left Smiley Alley and was walking past the tar pit when a stone hit him on the head. It wasn't very sore, but when Urgum saw who had thrown it, it was very irritating. A very tall, skinny savage had appeared on top of a distant rock. His vest was made from an old dustbin and the ragged end of his trousers flapped round his pointy knees. "What's in the bag, then?" came his irritating squeaky voice. "Bag bag bag, what?"

He was a nappar, the scum of the Lost Desert. Urgum hated nappars, they were thieving cowards who only dared to attack in packs, and he wasn't too pleased that a single nappar had dared to face him alone. It must have been because for once Urgum hadn't got his axe, and besides, the nappar was a long way off. Pity. Having a good fight with a few nappars would be just the thing to take his mind off the baby situation.

"Come and have a look if you like," said Urgum, but he knew the lanky bandit wouldn't dare to approach him alone, axe or no axe.

"Goo bah bah goo bah," came an urgent little message from the bag. A tiny hand was pointing back down the track behind them. Urgum turned to see a few more nappars had been quietly sneaking up while the first one distracted him. Their daggers were drawn, but as soon as he'd spotted them, they scurried back.

Urgum grinned at the little face in the bag. "Thanks for the warning!" he whispered. So a few more nappars had turned up, had they? With a bit of luck, he might just get a fight out of them after all.

"Bag bag bag, what?" The nappars had all started shouting now and their screechy voices were getting on his nerves. Urgum carefully put the bag down but as he reached inside, the nappars swapped their chanting for worried mutterings. What was the axeman going to produce? Maybe he had a folding axe and he could put it together, then chop them all to bits? Eeek! They were all just about to retreat in panic when…

goo goo bah

The nappars couldn't believe their eyes. Urgum was holding a little baby up for them to see. What was that about, then? He certainly couldn't attack them with it, so they all felt braver and crept forward to look. One of them felt so brave that he pointed at Urgum and shouted, "Nursemaid!" The others all gulped nervously. Urgum put the baby back safely, then stared a mean cold stare at them.

"What was that?" None of them dared reply. "It sounded like 'nursemaid'. Well?" The nappars were just about to turn and run when the axeman smiled. "I've not been called that before. Thanks!"

"Thanks?" muttered the nappars. They were utterly confused.

"Nursemaid's better than what I usually get called. It's usually something like 'fatty'."

"Fatty?" they repeated.

"Yes, fatty," said Urgum, patting his stomach. "Because I've been larding it up a bit, you see."

"Fatty fatty fatty!" gibbered the nappars. Suddenly they weren't so scared after all.

"Or you could try calling me 'smelly'," said Urgum. "If you don't believe me, get a noseful of these trousers."

One or two nappars crept even closer, still clutching their daggers. Being almost twice as tall as Urgum, they had to lean forward and bring their heads down to his height. Sure enough, "smelly" was a very good name for Urgum. They grinned and beckoned the others to join them.

"Smelly smelly smelly!"

"And then of course sometimes my wife calls me 'green eyes', because I've got these lovely green eyes, don't you think?"

"Eyes? Green eyes. Lovely green eyes. Lovely."

Urgum was standing in front of the bag, and by now the nappars were all bending down to get a good look at his lovely green eyes.

"So that's all the usual names," he said. "Fatty, smelly, green eyes … but do you know what the cleverest people call me?"

"What what what?" gibbered the nappars. Urgum gave them a chummy smile. Every single one of their puggy faces was within easy punching reach. Some days it was almost too easy.

"They call me ...

"URGUM THE AXEMAN!"

WHAMMBAMCRUNCH ZOKKABLATT

Urgum's fists and boots laid into the ragged bandits so fast and so hard that they didn't even have time to remember that they had their daggers out. They staggered, stumbled and scrambled away as fast as they could, all except one. The nappar that had first called out "nursemaid" had crept behind Urgum and had picked up the bag by the handles. Urgum snatched hold of it just in time, and sank his sharpened teeth into the nappar's wrist until he hit bone. The nappar released the bag and fell whimpering to the ground.

"Sorry about that," said Urgum. "I know I should have chopped your hand clean off, but my axe is having a day off. In fact, now I think of it, you were right in the first place. Today I'm not Urgum the Axeman – I am Urgum the Nursemaid."

Goo goo google google!

The baby certainly thought it was hilarious, even if the nappar was too busy howling to see the funny side. The bandit had just about got himself on all fours ready to crawl away when Urgum thought of something else funny to do. Urgum set the bag down and positioned it so that the baby would get a good view.

"Watch what I do now, you'll love this!" said Urgum. He ran up and swung his great boot hard into the nappar's bony bottom. The lanky bandit flew through the air, his arms and legs thrashing around like snakes in a frying pan, and then he landed in the tar pit with a juicy ...

SQUELCH!

It had all been marvellous fun and had kept them both laughing until Sacrifice Rock was in sight, but then, for some reason, Urgum actually began to feel a bit glum. The baby started to whimper.

"Cheer up, little friend," said Urgum. "There's no time for any of that. We're here!"

The rock was a harsh slab of white marble standing out on its own in the middle of the sand. Four heavy bolts had been driven into the corners, and each one was linked to a thick metal chain with manacles on the end.

"This place brings back memories," said Urgum, trying to sound jolly. "Mungoid and me used to play here for hours when we were kids. We'd ambush a savage from another tribe and clamp them on here, then

58

we'd wait to see what turned up. Sometimes it would be a pack of sandbadgers, other times it might be a sabre-toothed skunk or a few snakes. Once we even had a dragon! That was awesome. It shot one big blast of fire from its mouth and by the time the smoke had cleared, all that was left were a few bones and fingernails."

Bah wah goo wah!

Urgum found himself wondering what else he could say to cheer the baby up. High overhead, two ragged black shapes were circling.

"Look who's come to see you!" said Urgum. "It's our pet vultures, Djinta and Percy. Don't worry, they never eat live meat, so they won't peck at you until you're … well, until you're…"

Urgum couldn't finish what he was saying. He never thought he'd feel this way, but he had to admit that sometimes being a barbarian simply wasn't fun. He looked at the sun glaring off the white slab. He looked up at the vultures. He looked over to some distant trees. His savage senses prickled as he felt countless unblinking eyes watching from the shadows. Eyes that were connected to claws and teeth, no doubt.

He looked at the bag.

Bah wah wah.

Urgum gulped. He was deeply ashamed of what he was about to do, but deep down in his barbarian soul, he knew it was for the best.

Baby Talk

Urgum's savage senses had been right. While he was standing by Sacrifice Rock, he was being watched, but it wasn't just by creatures hiding in the trees. Up in the Hallowed Halls of Sirrus, the barbarian gods were in the middle of doing the washing-up, but had stopped to look down from the window to see what he was doing.

"A sacrifice!" exclaimed Tangal excitedly. "Urgum hasn't sent us a sacrifice for ages. We used to get a slaughtered bull every now and then. That was fun."

"Fun?" said Tangor doubtfully. "A bit of roast bull was OK on the first day, but the next day we'd have bull pie followed by bull casserole followed by bull omelettes, then bull soup, bull wellington, bull curry, bull sandwiches, bull and custard, bull ice cream … and before we'd had time to finish it, he'd go and sacrifice another one. I hate bull."

"Well, if he's got a bull in that bag, it's a very small one," sighed Tangal. She stuck her hands back into the sink and popped a few bubbles moodily. One of the frustrations of being a god is that even though you can trigger earthquakes and whip up tornados, it still doesn't get you out of doing the dishes.

"It's not any sort of bull," laughed Tangor. "Look!"

Far down below, Urgum was lifting the baby out of the bag.

"A baby?" said Tangal. "What are we going to do with that?"

"We could teach it to do the washing-up!"

This made Tangal grin with delight, until she spotted something outside flying towards them. It was a giant stork with a bulging nappy dangling from its beak.

"What's that thing doing?" she gasped.

"I don't know," admitted Tangor. "But I hope it's not stopping here."

But sure enough, when the stork reached the patch of cloud outside their door, it lowered its feet and landed.

Fplip fplop

Carefully it dipped its head and released the corners of the nappy, which opened out on the cloud. Sitting on the nappy were three huge wobbly figures. The smallest of the three pushed himself up to his feet and then toddled unsteadily towards them. His oversized head was almost bald, with wide blue eyes, and he had a large dummy jammed in his mouth. Without waiting to be invited, he squeezed his way in through the door, which made two of the poppers on his blue romper suit burst open. There was a **BUMPH** as his huge padded bottom hit the floor, and there he sat, casually chewing on his dummy and staring at them.

Tangor and Tangal were worried. They were supposed to be two of the most ancient and mighty gods of the Lost Desert, but although this god wasn't even a teeny bit ancient, it was obvious he was a whole lot mightier. Just to make it even more obvious, he was a wearing a bib with the words "I'm the boss" written on it.

After an uncomfortably long silence, their visitor reached a chubby hand up and pulled the dummy out of his mouth, making a deep **PLOP** noise.

"You don't mind if I drool, do you?" he said in a low voice. Of course he wasn't actually waiting for permission, he just let his lower lip hang down and a long syrupy drip slowly found its way to the floor.

"Who are you?" asked Tangor and Tangal.

"We are the baby gods," came the reply. "It's our job to protect our believers' interests."

"What interests?"

"Some of our little believers don't get treated so well during their time down below. It's our job to make sure that they are treated considerably better up here. Am I making myself CLEAR?"

"Why can't you look after your own babies?"

"Because … we're babies! We don't look after, we get looked after. So if you are blessed with the arrival of one

64

of our little believers, you will look after him."

"But we've never looked after a baby."

"That's why we're here, to give you a bit of practice. My name is Wedge."

"How do you do?" said Tangal. "My name is…"

"Not interested," yawned the baby. "The first rule you have to learn is that You Don't Matter. Now, then, it's time you met my associates."

The biggest and podgiest of the babies crawled in through the door, then rolled over on to his back, knocking the dining table over and crushing one of their chairs. All he was wearing was a nappy.

"Booty Bot here isn't walking yet, so he needs carrying," explained Wedge.

"Carrying?" gasped Tangal and Tangor.

"Yes, and feeding," said Wedge. "His favourite dinner is liquidized liver and prunes, and when I say dinner, I also mean breakfast, mid-morning snack, lunch time, afternoon snack, tea time, supper time, midnight feast and of course the early-hours feed, plus random supplementary top-ups as required. And then after that little lot, there's the nappy changes."

"OH NO!"

"Oh yes. Show them, Booty."

Booty Bot took a deep breath and pulled both his feet into his mouth. His face went scarlet as he turned up the pressure, ready to blast his nappy to bits. Tangor and Tangal dashed around him to get outside, only to find that the third huge baby had arrived in the doorway and blocked their escape.

"OK, we've got the message," said Tangor. "We'll make sure Urgum's baby gets the right food and clean nappies."

"But that's just the easy bit," said Wedge. "Now meet Daisybelle."

The third baby bottom-shuffled her way in. She had a little pink ribbon tied in the curls at the top of her head, a little spotty dress and gorgeous little white knitted booties.

"Aw!" said Tangal. "She is a beauty."

"I'm glad you see it that way," said Wedge. "Because Daisybelle is teething."

Daisybelle smiled to show her gums, then she grabbed the table and bit it as hard as she could. The tabletop splintered, her eyes opened wide in alarm and she let forth the most almighty

At first Tangor and Tangal just clamped their hands over their ears. It was so loud that they knew it would be over in a short time.

EEEEEEEEEEEEE...

They knew it couldn't last for ever.

EEEEEEEEEEEEE...

Actually it turned out that it was lasting for ever.

Tangor dangled things in front of Daisybelle and Tangal pulled funny faces, but it was useless. A waterfall of tears and snot was gushing down over her open mouth and congealing in a puddle of green slime on the little spotty dress.

EEEEEEEEEEEEEEEE...

The barbarian gods were desperate. Their usual way to deal with a problem was to swing an axe at it, but Booty Bot still had his feet in his mouth. If they made one false move, that straining nappy would erupt and they'd have to find somewhere else to live. With a sick feeling in their hearts, they knew that there was only one way to stop the noise.

"There, there," they both said. Trying to ignore the pain in their ears, they hugged the howling snot monster. It took a long time, but eventually:

EEEEEEEEEEEaM...

Tangor and Tangal peeled themselves away from the green slime which had glued them to Daisybelle's face and dress.

"There," said Wedge. "Now you've got the idea, we'll be on our way, but we will be looking in from time to time. Understood?"

Tangal and Tangor nodded meekly as Daisybelle and Booty Bot made their way back out to the blanket where the giant stork was waiting. Wedge hauled himself to his feet by grabbing on to the curtain and ripping it away from the wall in the process.

"There's just one more thing," he said, having a final look round. "This place is a dump. It stinks, there's dribble everywhere, you two are covered in snot, and all this broken stuff's dangerous."

"But you lot did that!"

"So? Get it seen to."

"But that's unfair!" shouted Tangal. "Why us?"

Wedge gave them a weary look. "Because, like I said before, You Don't Matter."

With that he plopped the dummy back in his mouth and tottered off to join the others.

Phantom Fears

It was night-time before Urgum got back to the cave. There was a burning torch on the wall outside and Divina was standing next to it waiting for him.

"Well?" she said with her left eyebrow raised to the challenging position.

"Well what?" snapped Urgum. "I did what was right."

"I do hope so," said Divina. She stared at him for a spooky moment, then stood aside to let him pass.

When he went in, he found the boys were all sitting round the fire. He could feel their eyes all over him, but if they had thought he was going to weaken and bring the baby back, they were wrong. Ruinn, the skinny son, looked sick and angry. Robbin, the biggest son, looked weepy and angry. The twins, Rekk and Rakk, looked surprised and angry. Raymond's bags all piled up in the corner looked piled up and angry. The seventh son looked … well, who cares? The only son who didn't look angry was Ruff, the eldest, who prided himself on being a mini-version of his father. He was sitting upright with his arms folded importantly.

"Well done, Father," he said. "The future of the tribe cannot depend on the life of one small child."

"Ah, shaddup!" shouted Ruinn and, along with the twins, he immediately leapt on Ruff and gave him a half-hearted pounding. Urgum wasn't naturally a sensitive type, but if the boys were so upset that they couldn't even be bothered to beat Ruff up properly, then he knew something had to be wrong.

"I do hope you're not all sulking about that baby," said Urgum, putting on his stern-dad voice. "You're all supposed to be merciless barbarians, but when it really comes down to a bit of nitty gritty, as usual you leave the dirty work to me. Well, the matter's dealt with, job done, so get over it."

Molly came out of the kitchen with a tray of dripping crocodile tails and shoved them at Urgum. "You didn't get any lunch," was all she said, then she stood back with her left eyebrow raised just like her mother's. Urgum chomped away, feeling very awkward, especially as everybody was watching him in complete silence. (Well, it would have been complete silence if Urgum hadn't been eating a pile of crocodile tails. But if you don't count SLOOP BOILK SLOBBER GLOBBLE MULB noises, then yes, it was complete silence.)

"Thank you, Molly," he said, finishing with a polite burp. He spat out a bony tail tip and was just wiping his hands on Ruinn's hair when the night outside echoed with a tiny scream.

WAH!

"Did you hear that?" said Robbin. They all stared at the cave entrance in terror.

"NO!" said Urgum abruptly. "Right, time for bed, you lot."

WAH AHA...

"There it goes again!" said Ruinn, his jaw quivering in fear.

"I knew it," gasped Robbin. "It's the baby phantom, come back to haunt us."

"This is all your fault, Ruff," accused Ruinn. "You forced Dad to take that poor kid away."

"M-me?" said Ruff, his face as white as sheet. "I was just upholding barbarian traditions."

"Enough!" Urgum shifted uncomfortably. "You heard NOTHING."

"You seem to be sweating a lot, Dad," said Robbin. "Are you sure you didn't hear it?"

"Absolutely," said Urgum, wiping his brow.

WAH

"And I didn't hear that one either," said Urgum.

The boys all turned on Ruff. "If that little boy comes back as a gjuntot, we all know who he's going to come for," said Robbin.

"He'll have wings like a bat," said Rekk.

"And metal teeth and claws to rip your flesh away," said Rakk.

"NO!" wailed Ruff, and he dashed away to the boys' bedroom, where he could curl up and hide under the safety of his bearskin blanket. Only it wasn't that safe, as all the other boys ran through to jump on him and make flying-baby-with-metal-teeth noises. At least they were beating him up properly now, thought Urgum. Molly came to take the empty tray.

"So you're not bothered by ghosty noises, then?" asked Urgum. He was having trouble keeping his breath steady.

"Why should I be?" Molly glared at him in the firelight. "I'm not the one that left a baby out there, all on his own, to DIE."

Urgum's knees were shaking, he was feeling hot and cold at the same time, but why? Surely it couldn't be

fear? Urgum was so tough that the thought of being frightened terrified him. He staggered outside to clear his head and found Divina looking out into the blackness of the basin.

"Something bothering you?" she said.

"No," said Urgum defiantly.

"If you say so," said Divina. "But you're shaking and sweating."

"I'm not," Urgum lied.

"Well, you should be."

"I'm not scared of little silly ghosties."

"Maybe not, but you should be scared of upsetting Molly."

"Why?"

"Because she soaked all those crocodile tails in fire wasp tail sauce."

Even as she said it, Urgum could feel his face, tongue, throat, neck stomach and deep-down bottom bits starting to burn.

BLEAURGHHHHH!

Urgum had to gulp in as much air as he could. With

his mouth wide open, he ran around the bear pit three times, up the wall, off the wall, jumped right over the bone pile and ended up sitting in the lynching tree holding his tongue out with one hand while the other hand scraped the burning spikes off it with an old clam shell. From the cave entrance he saw Molly standing, watching him, unsmiling.

Urgum did not feel loved.

Bad Hair Night

The heavy wooden door across Grizelda the Grizly's cave entrance was shut and bolted for the night. Inside, the pink candles flickered by the golden mirror as Grizelda put her hair up, ready for bed. It had been a good day. Once the water had gone, she'd ridden out on her horse with her bow and arrows to see what she could get and had returned home with two red swans for tea, which was nice, but the main thing she'd got while she was out was a LOT of admiring glances. No wonder. When Grizelda was gliding along in her slinky armour with her flame-coloured hair lashing around her shoulders, there wasn't a male in the Lost Desert who didn't look round. One or two even dared to give a loud whistle, but a killer glance from the archer assassin soon taught them some manners. They knew that whistling was disrespectful and they could end up with an arrow through the nose. What they didn't know was that even though she gave them killer glances, Grizelda secretly loved being whistled at. It meant that a few sad souls were so smitten with her looks that they were prepared to risk getting an extra nostril just to catch her attention for a tiny instant.

At last all her precious hair was gathered on top of her head, so she carefully eased a soft yak-skin bag over it and fixed it in place with a few stout wooden pegs. The bag still had a few twiggy yak hairs sticking out. It might have looked ridiculous, but she couldn't risk any sand spiders coming to nest on her head while she was asleep, and besides, the door was bolted so no one would ever see it. It was just as well, because nobody would whistle if they caught her in that state, especially as she'd swapped her slinky armour for a comfortable old patched velvety nightshirt. She laid herself back on her bed and listened out for the soft reassuring night noises of the desert to usher her off to sleep.

SKRARKKK!

The relaxing sound of an ostrich claw scraping out the insides of an elephant snail.

GARREEK FSSSiSSS GARREEK

The gentle cries of two giant bats having a mid-air tug of war with a cobra.

RHOOON!

Ooh! thought Grizelda. There was one she hadn't heard for a while – the melodic tones of an anguished hippopotamus drowning in the tar pit.

It was all very sweet and soothing, but there was one

noise missing. Usually by now, the entire rock basin would be echoing with Mungoid the Ungoid's great rumbling snores. Although she was hardly friends with her next-door neighbour, it was always reassuring to know he was there. So where was he snoring now? Had he gone to snore next door to some other female savage? *Then I'll KILL her*, Grizelda promised herself which made her feel a lot better. She listened out again. No nice deep rumbly snores. Oh well. She closed her eyes and tried to kick off with a dream about marmalade ice cream and peach sauce when

WAH

Her eyes shot open. What was that? Grizelda hadn't heard anything like it before. Her palms sweated, her toes clenched. Had she just imagined it? Probably. So anyway, eyes closed, marmalade ice cream, peach sauce and ooh, how about a few chocolate wafers?

WAH-HA

She was out of bed and on her feet even before the ice cream had disappeared. The sound wasn't loud, but it was very close and it was making her brain rattle like a bag of pebbles.

WAH-AHA-AHA-WAAAAAAAH!

It was coming through the solid rock wall from Mungoid's cave. What could it be? Without thinking, she unbolted her door and, grabbing a long skinning knife, she dashed outside and ran round to look.

"There, there," came Mungoid's voice softly. "Uncle Mungoid's here. Time for sleepy pies."

Mungoid was sitting by his rock stove hugging a strange bluey-grey bundle. Grizelda realized it was one of his huge winter woolly socks and there was something wriggling inside it. "Shhh!" he said to the sock. "There's nothing to be afraid of." Then Mungoid looked up and saw the ghastly apparition with the nasty dagger hovering in the darkness outside.

"ARGHHHH! Begone, devil spirit!" In a panic, the great Ungoid rose to his feet and bared his huge clunking teeth. He did his best to control his knocking knees and yelled, "If you so much as touch the baby I'll have you banished for ever to the bottom of the bottomless blasted abyss of eternal badness, where you will be banished eternally for everly bottomly badly bannily abyss bottom blast ... with lots more even badder stuff like that."

That's when Grizelda realized that this wasn't one of those moments that she was ever going to be whistled at, in fact, she wasn't really decked out for public viewing at all. With a shriek she disappeared back into her cave, bolted the door, ripped off the nightshirt and the yak-skin bag and threw herself into her armour while combing out her hair as quickly as she possibly could. As soon as she had restored her usual whistledattedness, she took a deep breath, calmly unbolted her door and went to find Mungoid standing on guard outside his cave and peering around the dark rock basin in disbelief.

"Are you all right?" she asked as casually as she could. "I thought I heard something."

Mungoid laughed uneasily. "I've never seen anything like it," he said. "It was evil, hideous, some sort of desert spirt. A banshee or even gjuntot maybe."

"So you didn't recognize it?" asked Grizelda nervously.

"Nah!" said Mungoid, cheering up a bit. "I just put a really scary curse on it, and it screamed and flitted off."

"And you've no idea where it went?"

"Er … I think it flew away over Urgum's place."

"That's a relief," said Grizelda. "But why was it coming to get the baby?"

"Baby?" said Mungoid. "How did you know I had a baby in here?"

Erk! Grizelda had nearly given herself away. Mungoid wasn't holding the baby now, so how could she have known about it? She would have to think of a very clever answer if Mungoid wasn't to realize that the evil hideous spirit had actually been her.

"I guessed," she answered very cleverly.

"You *guessed*? I'm an Ungoid living alone in a cave in the Lost Desert, and yet you guessed that suddenly tonight somehow from somewhere I'd ended up looking after a baby?"

"Yes."

"Well, that must be the most amazing guess ever," said Mungoid. "You're right, but I hope nobody else guesses. It's supposed to be a secret."

Mungoid realized that having the baby was better than any chat-up line he could have thought of, so he took his chance and invited Grizelda in to sit by his stove with the little woollen bundle lying between them. He explained how ashamed Urgum had felt when he couldn't leave the baby on Sacrifice Rock, so he'd sneaked it back into Golgarth and asked Mungoid to look after it. By the time Mungoid had finished explaining, the little bundle was starting to get restless again.

WAAAAAAAH!

Mungoid carefully picked up the screaming child. He did his best to keep it wrapped in the great woolly sock, but it wasn't easy when there was such a violent protest going on. Tiny little hands and feet kept thrusting themselves out to grab and kick anything in reach and resisting his huge Ungoid fingers' delicate attempts to tuck them back in.

WAH-AH-AH-AAAAAAAH!

"It's not going to be a secret long it if keeps making that noise," said Grizelda.

"He must be hungry," said Mungoid. Wearily he struggled to his feet and started pacing up and down the cave, hugging the struggling bundle to his chest. Gradually the screams reduced to a muffled whimper.

WAAH-AH-aM-uMMMM-MMM

"Why don't you feed him?" demanded Grizelda.

"I've tried," said Mungoid. "But he doesn't seem to like bison rib bones and I haven't any milk. What do you think we should do?"

"*We?*" Grizelda immediately got up to go. "There's no *we* about this. Urgum gave him to you, not me. It's your problem."

"Oh," said Mungoid. "I see." For a brief moment he stopped in his tracks and immediately the violent protests started up again.

WAH-AHA-AHA-AHHH!

Once again Mungoid started to plod ponderously up and down his cave. Without looking round he said, "Sorry we woke you up then. Good night, Grizelda."

"Good night?" snapped Grizelda. "What's good about it? If he doesn't shut up, how will I sleep?"

"If he doesn't shut up, the others might find him and kill him," said Mungoid. "Then you'll be able to sleep as much as you like, won't you?"

Grizelda stood motionless in the cave entrance, biting her lip and feeling utterly rotten. Mungoid was still dragging his tired feet along the floor, waiting for the screams to turn back to whimpers again. He was completely ignoring her and she didn't blame him one little bit.

RHOOON!

Once again Grizelda heard the anguished noise coming from out across the dark desert, and it gave her an idea. "Mungoid?" she said softly. He didn't answer, he just plodded up to her, turned around and plodded back. "Listen to me, Mungoid. You keep going, I'm popping out to the tar pit, but I'll be back."

This time he did stop and he even gave her a curious look. "The tar pit? This time of night?"

The bundle twitched and took a deep breath, ready for the next scream.

"Yes, but I'll be back as soon as I can."

"How soon's that?"

"I don't know," she said. "It's the first time I've tried to milk a hippopotamus in the dark."

On the other side of Golgarth Basin, Divina was the only one still awake. She had been lying on the bed for ages, while next to her Urgum had shifted and twitched until the worst effects of the fire wasp tail sauce had worn off. Of course she known all along that the cries they'd heard had come from Mungoid's cave, even if Urgum had been too proud to admit what he'd done. Divina rolled over towards her husband and gave him a great big kiss right on the nose. She'd always trusted him to do the right thing, even if he hadn't a clue what the right thing was.

The Morning After the Night Before

Early next morning, the first orange skewers of sunlight blazed down over the top of the cragg wall and sliced through the gloom of Golgarth Basin. Thanks to the recent rains, a thick haze had gathered overnight, and from it emerged a dawn chorus of squelchy noises as a parade of fat white slugs hurried away to hide in the cold murky shadows under the rocks.

Grizelda the Grizly twitched, yawned and murmured "strawberry topping", but she was leaning against something too warm and comfortable to bother waking up properly. She snuggled up again, shouted, "Don't forget the crushed nuts", and dozed off back to sleep.

A big eye opened right next to her head and swivelled round in astonishment. Mungoid couldn't believe that Grizelda was sitting beside him, in his very own cave, asleep on his shoulder. Was it a dream? Was it real? Mungoid didn't care so long as it kept going. Very slowly, so

as not to wake her, he closed his eye as quietly as he could.

Meanwhile one of the fat white slugs had got lost and was working its way up Grizelda's leg. "Oh, all right, but this is my last bowlful," mumbled Grizelda sleepily, and she reached forward to grab the cherry off the top of her five-flavour special. As she brought it up to her mouth, it wrapped itself around her finger. Her eyes blinked open and the cherry turned into a white slug and she wasn't in the Parad-Ice Cream Parlour any more. Instead she was leaning against Mungoid, she was covered in bruises and splashes of tar, and she was clutching a half-full cup of hippopotamus milk. She leapt up in panic, bolted outside, dashed into her own cave and slammed the door shut.

What? How? Why? Well, whatever had been going on, nobody had seen her. And thank goodness Mungoid had been asleep. If he knew anything about it, he'd only think he'd been dreaming. Or at least, that's what he'd think if he knew what was good for him.

Secret Milk

When Urgum woke up the next day, he really wished he hadn't. He didn't even bother opening his eyes. He was still feeling extremely delicate in the guts department, but even worse, he knew that everybody hated him.

It wouldn't have been so bad if it was just some of his savage friends that hated him because that would have been the perfect excuse for a massive gruesome fight. Urgum loved any sort of fighting, but fighting people who hated him was the best because when he won he could teach them a lesson by chopping them into little bits and feeding them to the vultures. Ha! That way they all learnt that they shouldn't go round hating Urgum. Oh yes, after that they realized that liking Urgum was by far the most sensible option. That's why over the years the Lost Desert had become dotted with bits of vulture poo that all agreed what a lovely bloke Urgum was.

But this day was different because it was his family that all hated him, and chopping them all up to make them like him just didn't seem right. Urgum was going to have to put up with all the bad things about being hated without being able to appreciate any of the good things. No wonder he didn't want to wake up.

"Hello, Father."

Urgh. Somebody was talking to him.

"Are you awake?"

"No."

"Just wanted you to know, you did the right thing casting that baby out yesterday. I'm proud of you."

Urgum prised an eyelid open. His eldest son, Ruff, was standing by the bed looking very smug. Pity. If there was one member of his family who needed feeding to the vultures, it was Ruff.

"Do you hate me?" asked Urgum hopefully.

"Not me, Father!" Ruff grinned. "We're the only true

barbarians in the place. You and me have to stick together."

Urgum felt even iller. The last thing he needed was to be stuck to Ruff, so with that revolting thought in the back of his mind, he decided to get up and face the rest of them. He stumbled along the corridor, clutching on to the rocky wall for support. The lingering smell of crocodile tail still hung in the air, making his stomach shrivel up and crack like a walnut. He didn't think anything could have been more puke-worthy, until he got to the main part of the cave. All his other sons were lined up, smiling big lovey-dovey smiles at him. It was totally horrible.

"What's up with you lot?" he groaned.

"It's all right," they all said, tapping their noses with their fingers. "We know!"

Urgum turned on Ruff, who had sauntered in behind him. "What do they know?" he demanded.

"I don't know," said Ruff.

"But we do," said all the others. "It's a secret, isn't it, Dad?"

Urgum was bewildered, and it wasn't helped when Divina came out of the kitchen and gave him a saucy wink, the sort of wink that makes your socks stick to your feet. Finally Molly came out carrying a large jug.

"We thought you might like some nice milk, Dad," she said.

"MILK?" Suddenly Urgum realized the true evilness of their plan. He hated milk. What with his dodgy guts, the sickly smiles and the milk, it was obvious that they were trying to make him so sick that his entire body would turn inside out. "Milk? Do I look like the sort of person who drinks milk? I never drink milk. I'm a barbarian, I drink hot blood with toenails in it. Not milk. It's too milky. Yuk."

"Steady on, Dad," said Molly. "It's only milk."

"Father does not drink milk," declared Ruff. "Milk is only fit for babies."

"Yes," said Urgum. "That's right. Milk is for babies."

To his concern, he saw all the boys nodding in agreement and smiling and tapping their noses at him and muttering odd things like, "Ah, yes, babies, milk is for babies, absolutely, babies drink milk…"

"Look, Dad," said Molly. "You know you like milk…"

"I DON'T!"

"Well, actually you secretly do, but if you want to drink it in secret, why don't you take it over to Mungoid's?"

Once again the boys were nodding, all apart from Ruff. "And exactly why would Father want to take milk over to Mungoid's?" he demanded with his arms folded in a righteous way. "Milk is for babies."

But Urgum was having a silent think. Milk? Mungoid? Babies?

PING!

Urgum had the most incredibly clever idea.

"You know what?" said Urgum. "I've just realized. I could really do with a secret drink of milk."

"Really?" asked Divina.

"Yes, really," Urgum whispered secretly to everybody. "You see, actually I just remembered it's my favourite drink."

"Dad!" Ruff was horrified. "Barbarians never drink milk."

"Well, actually they do," explained Urgum. "But only in secret. And I'll tell you who else drinks secret milk. Ungoids."

"You mean like Mungoid the Ungoid?"

"Absolutely. If it comes to secret milk-drinking, Mungoid's your man. In fact, I might just take some milk over to Mungoid's."

And so, to Ruff's horror, Urgum set off across the

basin to Mungoid's carrying the jug of milk, with Molly skipping along behind him.

"Go away, Molly," said Urgum. "This is a secret drink of milk that nobody knows about."

"Yeah, right, Dad," grinned Molly.

Urgum looked at her hopelessly. "Why does nobody believe me?"

"Mum heard the baby crying from Mungoid's last night. She told me this morning."

"I hope you didn't tell any of the others!" said Urgum, horrified.

"Me? I'd never betray you," said Molly. "I didn't tell a single person apart from Robbin. But he only told Ruinn, who only told the twins, who only told Raymond, who only told the other one."

"So nobody told Ruff, then?"

"Of course not. It's a secret."

When they got to Mungoid's cave, the great Ungoid himself was slumped fast asleep against the wall with a huge grin on his face. He was obviously having a fabulous dream about something.

$$goo\ goo\ bah$$

A little hand stuck out from the bluey-grey bundle on

Mungoid's lap. Molly was about to squeal with delight, but Urgum clamped his hand over her mouth. Molly understood – let Mungoid sleep on! Very carefully Molly eased the baby from Mungoid's grasp, then Urgum took off his hat and left it there in place. When Mungoid woke up, he'd know where the baby had gone.

They quietly collected the baby's bag that was lying in a corner and were stepping out of the cave when they saw Ruff on the other side of the basin peering across at them suspiciously. Molly quickly pulled Urgum back inside. Moments later Urgum came out again, cradling the bag and whispering into it.

"There, there. You get your sleep, you'll be all right now."

Ruff marched up to him indignantly. "You were supposed to leave that thing on Sacrifice Rock."

"Shhh!" said Urgum.

"Why?" snapped Ruff. "How come all the others knew you'd brought it back and not me? I'm supposed to be your number one son, it's just not fair! That brat keeps making me look like a complete plop."

"So what?" said Urgum.

"It's your fault! You let me down. What kind of a barbarian are you if you can't cast a little baby out? You said you would."

"It's not that easy," said Urgum.

"Why not?" demanded Ruff. "It's only a baby."

"Is that what you think?" said Urgum slowly. He held the bag out towards Ruff. "Then if you want it done, you do it."

Ruff gulped. He hadn't quite expected that. Behind him he could hear his brothers hissing and jeering, so he had no choice but to take it.

The bag was heavier than Ruff had imagined, which didn't help, but so long as the baby didn't make a noise, he'd be able to pretend it wasn't for real. He'd just play along with being tough until they all gave in and admitted that he was the only real barbarian among them. Big respect would come his way. Oh yes!

"Dad, you can't let him!" shouted Robbin from the cave.

"My number one son must have a chance to prove he is a true barbarian sometime," said Urgum solemnly.

"Can't he just grow a beard and burp a bit?" shouted Ruinn.

"Enough!" said Urgum. He raised his voice mightily.

"RUFF, GO FORTH, MY SON.

FOR WHEN YOU RETURN IT WILL BE

KNOWN

WHETHER OR NOT YOU are indeed a

TRUE BARBARIAN

OR JUST a COMPLETE PLOP."

Ruff went forth. Of course there were a few shouts from his brothers such as "Don't forget the phantom" and "Look, his little legs are shaking", but that only made Ruff walk faster across the basin to the crack in the wall. Without looking back, he hurried past Olk, and soon he and the bag had disappeared off into the desert beyond.

A glum silence fell across the whole of Golgarth Basin. Even the ostriches stopped scratching. Molly walked over from Mungoid's looking shocked.

"I feel so sick," she said. "I never thought he'd do it."

"Neither did we," said the boys, their hearts heavy as stone.

"I didn't think he'd do it either," said Urgum.

"Did you think he'd do it?" Molly was talking to the bluey-grey bundle she was carrying. **goo goo bah** came the answer.

Up in the Halls of Sirrus, there was a huge sigh of relief. When Ruff had first set off, Tangor and Tangal had been in a blind panic. If the baby had really been heading for Sacrifice Rock, it could well have ended up living with them. They hadn't forgotten Wedge's threats, they could still feel the pain from Daisybelle's teething scream and smell Booty Bot's nappy, and that had only been a quick visit! How would they cope with having a baby with them for ever?

"Molly saved us this time," said Tangal. "But we've got to make sure that can't happen again. That baby must never be left out on Sacrifice Rock, or anywhere else for that matter."

They looked down and saw that Ruff had already reached Smiley Alley, but then a glint of sunlight from the cragg wall caught their attention. Strange! It had come off Olk's blade. Usually the mighty sentry held it motionless across his shoulder, but Olk was waving goodbye to the bag.

Tangor nudged Tangal excitedly. "I think I've got it! We need to get down there and reprogramme Olk."

Wrong Wrong Wrong

Ruff had stomped out of the basin past Olk without looking back because he knew the others would be feeling sad and pathetic (wrong). They would be admiring what an awesome barbarian he was (even wronger), and one thing he knew for absolute certain: right now none of them would be laughing at him (oh, so *very* wrong).

STOMP STOMP STOMP

Of course Ruff had no intention of lugging the heavy

bag all the way out to Sacrifice Rock, he just had to look like he meant it. He knew they wouldn't let anything happen to their precious baby, and it wouldn't be long before they called out, begging him to come back. And he was really going to make them beg, oh yes! He'd show them that true barbarians weren't to be messed about with.

Ruff stomped down Smiley Alley and felt the skulls all grinning at him. Why wasn't anybody calling him yet? Once he got past the end it would be too late. He had to slow down, but he didn't want to make it obvious to anyone watching, so he just took smaller and smaller steps. Smaller and smaller … soon he was just stomping his feet up and down on the same bit of ground. The skull next to him wasn't just grinning, it was laughing its head off. And that's a very difficult thing for a skull to do, so something must have been *very* funny.

"RUFF!"

At last! Ruff swung round and saw his brothers waving down at him from the watchtower on top of the cragg wall. "Forget it," he shouted. "I'm not coming back!"

"Oh yes, you are coming back," they all laughed. "Look in the bag."

The howls of laughter from the tower got even worse when Ruff stuck his hand in and pulled out Mungoid's breakfast – a long, fat hippopotamus tongue.

"Ha ha ha, you BIG PLOP!"

"RIGHT!" he yelled, waving the tongue. "Form a queue to DIE because I'm coming BACK."

"Ha ha ha! Told you so!"

STOMP STOMPY STOMP STOMP

By the time Ruff got back to the entrance, he thought

his stomping had got so angry and scary that even Olk wouldn't dare to stop him. This thought was also wrong. In fact, it was so wrong that the wrongness of it could have been served up with chips and a splash of wrong sauce.

"Password," uttered the giant sentry.

"Cheese knife," said Ruff.

"WRONG!"

"Oh don't be silly," said Ruff. He was about to barge past but something swooped down towards his face. He threw himself to the ground just as Olk's blade managed to scalp the back of his head. "What are you doing?" demanded Ruff. "It's me!"

Of course, Ruff had no way of knowing that deep inside Olk's brain, two tiny little chaos spiders had been hard at work hacking into the password recognition matrix.

"So far so good," said

Tangal, adding a few final strands to a nerve web. "He seems to be rejecting the original password, but let's try it again. Hit the reset."

Tangor scuttled over to a big red neuron. He only meant to give it one kick, but he'd forgotten he had eight legs, so he accidentally gave it a few more. Impulses flashed and buzzed along the new weblines and Olk's mouth jerked open.

"P ... P ... PAH ... PASS ... PASSWORD ... SWURD ... URD."

"Cheese knife?" said Ruff, but this time he was standing well back when

"WRONG!"

boomed out and the gruesome blade swung round again.

The boys had arrived behind Olk.

"We thought you were coming back to kill us," said Ruinn.

"Yeah, go on!" said Rekk.

"Ooh, we're really scared," said Rakk.

"I WAS going to kill you but I can't get IN," shouted Ruff.

"LOSER! HA HA HA HA HA HA!"

Ruff stamped his foot and pulled his reddest face and

waved the big tongue again. He knew he was losing his temper and looking stupid and pathetic … but then to his astonishment he realized the other sons weren't laughing at him any more. They were just standing and staring at him in horror. Ruff couldn't believe it. He waved the tongue again.

"Don't do that!" said Robbin. "Really, don't do it!"

"I'll do it if I want to," grinned Ruff, waving the tongue round his head. The boys all gasped, and even Olk's sword trembled slightly. It was the best moment of Ruff's life.

"Look behind you," said Ruinn.

"I'm not falling for that one!" said Ruff. "How stupid do you think I am?"

"No, really," said Robbin. "Stop waving that thing and look behind you!"

"You're not fooling me, you LOSERS!" Ruff was still waving the tongue and grinning nastily when the large black shadow that had been cruising up Smiley Alley finally fell across him. There was a rush of air and a thrash of giant wings.

GALL-ULP

The boys all dashed out to watch as the peligantuan soared away across the desert. Maybe it had only intended to snatch the tongue, but Ruff had got scooped up in the beak pouch too.

Inside Golgarth Basin, Urgum was fixing a wooden box with leather straps on to the back of his horse.

"What's that?" asked Divina.

"It's a baby seat so I can take Googoobah out on raids and battles," explained Urgum. "You've got to have a baby seat to keep them safe, you know."

"MUM, DAD!" The boys were all shouting from outside the crack in the wall. "Ruff's been swallowed by a giant bird."

"Just ignore him," replied Urgum. "He's always showing off."

"Come on!" cried Divina. "It could be serious."

Urgum and Divina dashed out to see a tiny speck disappearing in the far sky. The boys were already arguing about who they should hate the most now that Ruff was gone.

"Stop that!" snapped Divina, who was quite upset. "You're all my little precious babies, and never forget that Ruff will always be your brother. I want you to go on hating him just like you've always done."

"Yes, Mum," they said, but it wasn't going to be much fun hating Ruff if he wasn't there. Meanwhile Urgum was trying to get back inside, but there seemed to be a problem.

"Look here, Olk, my old mate, enough's enough. I need to get in, so no more jokes."

"PASSWORD."

"I've already said it. Cheese knife."

"WRONG!"

The long blade twitched menacingly. Urgum skipped back out of the way, nearly knocking Divina over. "Have you changed the password, dear?" he asked.

"No," said Divina. "Maybe you're not saying it right. Olk, listen to me. *Cheese knife.*"

"WRONG!"

Now they were all getting worried. The only person who usually changed the password was Divina because she was the only person who had a hope of telling Olk what to do. Unless ... it might have been Molly!

"MOLLY!" they all shouted.

Molly came out, clutching Googoobah in his big sock.

"Did you change the password?"

"You mean cheese knife?" said Molly.

"WRONG!"

This was awful. Now they were all stuck outside. The bundle in Molly's arms started to wriggle impatiently.

"Sorry, baby," said Molly, "but Uncle Olk isn't letting us back in!" A little hand wriggled free of Mungoid's sock and pointed at Olk.

goo goo bah

"ENTER!"

"Enter?" gasped Urgum. "Why?"

goo goo bah

"ENTER!"

said Olk again.

Ruinn had been thinking hard. "Somehow the password's changed to goo goo bah," he said, walking up to Olk. "Let me try it. Goo goo bah."

"WRONG!"

By this time Olk was clearly getting bored of shouting "wrong", so he gave his blade a big swish round to go with it, making Ruinn dive backwards.

"I think I've got it," said Molly. "Olk will only accept

the new password from Googoobah. That means we'll never be able to get into Golgarth again without him!"

Inside Olk's brain, the two chaos spiders gave a little cheer. Thanks to Molly, Urgum and the others knew that whatever else might happen, they had to keep the baby safe. Feeling rather pleased with themselves, Tangor and Tangal dematerialized back up to Sirrus, leaving their weblines quietly sparking and humming away. Their plan had worked perfectly, and it seemed as though their baby-minding nightmare was over.

Meanwhile Urgum and everybody were all bunched together very tightly in front of Olk. "Stick close to us," said Molly, holding the baby up. "We're going in."

goo goo bah

"ENTER!"

Very warily they moved forward. "Gently does it," said Urgum, as they carefully shuffled under the blade. It trembled slightly but it didn't look like it was going to swoop round. Then again, none of them were absolutely certain about that. "Maybe he should just say one more for luck…"

goo goo bah

The Carved Coin

Divina was in the cave watching Urgum, who was lying on the floor with Googoobah bouncing up and down on his great stomach.

"That's it!" Urgum was saying. "Now, when you wrestle a dragon, you have to flip him on to his back just like that, then you stick a dagger

in the soft bit under his mouth. Oh, and keep your head back because they don't half spurt blood do dragons, and it tastes vile."

goo goo bah

"That's enough quality time for now," smiled Divina. "It's time for Googoobah's nap."

"Me too," said Urgum, yawning. "I'd forgotten how hard it was being a dad, and I've been dadding all morning."

"Urgie, we need to talk about that," said Divina.

"About what?" said Urgum, not really listening.

"Urgie, we don't know where he came from, but he's not ours."

Urgum propped himself up on his elbow and flashed her a cross glance. "Why not? Ruff's gone, and he's here. It's a good swap. He's mine until anybody else can prove different."

"When we found him, there was something else in the bag." Divina opened a small pouch that hung from a cord around her neck and tipped a few small objects out on to her hand. Urgum pointed at a tiny white lump.

"Aw! It's the first tooth that Rekk lost," he said, smiling fondly. "Rakk could throw a mean punch even as a baby."

Divina picked out a small flat piece of green metal. "This is what came with Googoobah."

"That's one of those money coin things," said Urgum, lying back again. "Big deal."

"It's more than that," said Divina. The coin had been roughly cut in half, leaving a jagged edge. "It's a kisskey. Somebody will be keeping the other half safe. Usually two people in love keep them."

"Wahey!" exclaimed Urgum. "You mean Gubbs has got a bit of wallop wallop woof woof going on? Go, boy, go!"

"Don't be silly," said Divina. "Googoobah must have been left by somebody in desperate trouble. Somebody who wanted us to keep him safe until the day they can take him back."

"Oh," said Urgum. "No wallop wallop woof woof then."

"No," said Divina. "But Urgie, you have to understand that one day somebody might come along with the matching kisskey…"

"Yes, dear," said Urgum, hugging Googoobah to his

chest. "And you have to understand that I'll kill them."

"Don't be so selfish," said Divina. "We're lucky to enjoy the time we have with him. But when the day comes…"

"…Yeah, I know." Urgum sighed. Divina was right, but then she was always right. Boring boring boring, but Urgum hadn't time to waste worrying about that. He had a lot more dadding to do. "OK, Gubbs, here's what you do when two elephants have got their trunks round your legs and they're trying to pull you apart…"

PART ONE AND A HALF

A DATE IS MADE

PARAD-ICE CREAM PARLOUR

A Date is Made

Mungoid yawned, shifted, stretched, got to his feet and automatically started plodding up and down his cave, rocking Urgum's hat to stop it crying. *Eh? Urgum's hat? Ah!* thought Mungoid. With a sigh of relief he collapsed on to the floor again, and reached up to scratch something that was itching on his neck. He pulled his finger away to see the something had got wedged under his fingernail. It was a black blob with a long red hair attached to it. *What? Eh? Oooh!*

It was one of Grizelda's hairs, but how had it got stuck to him with a drop of tar? That strange dream he'd had last night must have been really real! It didn't make sense, but Mungoid didn't care. *It was one of Grizelda's fabulous hairs.* He carefully hung it over a little rock spike sticking out of his cave wall, then he couldn't help pulling the ends to make it slide backwards and forward. He was admiring how the light glanced off it when

PTiNK!

The end of the rock spike fell to the floor. The hair had cut right through it. Suddenly Mungoid felt sheepish. He couldn't keep this fantastic strand of hair, it was Grizelda's. He had to return it.

At the same time next door, Grizelda had been scrubbing off the tar splodges and was trying to make herself look as normal as possible. She started combing through her hair but immediately knew that something was wrong! She stuck her fingers into her scalp and felt around very carefully. Her worst fears were realized – there was a hair missing! She cast her mind back to the night before. Oh no…

Just then a polite cough came from the doorway.

"Good morning, Grizelda," said Mungoid. "I found something of yours."

Mungoid was holding out the single red hair.

"WHERE DID YOU GET IT?"

"I've no idea," lied Mungoid. "It was just … lying around."

Grizelda knew that Mungoid must have known how he'd got it, but he wasn't letting on. He was such a sweetie. If only he had just a bit more nerve – what did she have to do?

"Why would I want one hair back?" she retorted.

"It's yours."

"So? I'm not falling for that. I know you're after something."

"After something? Like what?"

"Like I've got to go out with you on a date or something," said Grizelda.

"Oh, I wouldn't dream of asking that."

"Ha!" snapped Grizelda. "Don't you try to kid me by playing the big softie. OK, you win, I'll come out with you. Parad-Ice Cream Parlour it is. Sometime in the next day or two, time to be confirmed. OK? Happy now? Got what you wanted?"

Still clutching the hair, Mungoid toddled back to his cave with a big confused smile on his face. Oh yes, he'd got what he'd ALWAYS wanted, he just wasn't quite sure how or why he'd got it.

PART TWO

THE RATTLE BATTLE

The High Life

Ruff didn't recognize Golgarth Basin until he realized the line of tiny white dots leading up to it were the skulls along Smiley Alley. It was the most brain-tingling thing he had ever seen. Over on the horizon, a few lazy fumes were drifting up from the Forgotten Crater, while the other way he could see the towers and turrets of the Laplace Estates and beyond that, the shimmering unreality of the Upside Down Lake.

He was standing with his feet in the bottom of the peligantuan's pouch and peering out of the giant bird's beak as it soared and swooped over the Lost Desert. Since he'd been scooped up, the bird had only landed a couple of times. That's when it had tipped its head back and tried to swallow him down its smelly dark neck hole, but Ruff had kicked, punched and wriggled so hard that it had given up.

It had crossed his mind to try and sneak out while the bird rested, but why? What for? Everybody hated him, ignored him, teased him. Why would he want to go back to that when he could fly round the desert? At last he was able to look down on everybody rather than the other way round. That's why Ruff had decided to stay where he was for as long as it lasted.

Mixing it with the Knitter Boys

Pop pop pop, went Divina. Oh yes indeed, Divina was having a marvellous time popping into market, popping into shops and popping into drink cherry water with other ladies. Having a new baby had changed her life, and given her some thrillingly exciting things to discuss with Molly.

"Aren't those little woolly booties nice?" Divina would say as they passed a knitwear stall.

"Yeah, nice, Mum," Molly would reply. "Wow."

"Oh, and aren't those little furry earmuffs nice?" Divina

would gush as they passed a rodent recycling booth.

"Tremendously nice. Wow again."

Molly wasn't quite so keen as her mother was on these outings, but she never complained because she wouldn't be heard over the barrage of moans, whinges, curses and general grief flowing from Urgum and the boys, who always came with them. Of course, Urgum would far rather have been charging round the desert with his sons shouting

YARGHHH,

picking fights, waving axes and hunting enormously dangerous animals, but Divina had banned him from taking Googoobah, and without Googoobah to say the password, Olk wouldn't let them back in. Therefore if Urgum and the others wanted to get out at all, they had to go where Divina went, and those were trips that involved lots of popping.

One morning they were all outside the Gossiperia Tonic Rooms. "We'll just pop in here," said Divina jollily.

There was an even bigger groan than usual. The Gossiperia was full of itchy chairs and little wobbly tables and people who held dainty goblets of cherry water with their little fingers sticking out. "Have we got to?" sulked Urgum.

"I'm meeting Glamora," said Divina. "She'll think you're very rude if you don't come in too."

"Then she's right," said Urgum. "We are very rude. Good old Glamora. I'd hate her to be wrong. We better not come in."

"URGUM!" The eyebrow was up.

"Help me here, chaps," whispered Urgum to his loyal sons.

PLIMP PLOMP PULLIMP

"Listen!" said Ruinn, holding his ear out towards the door. "They've got a harp player."

"Oh come on, Dad, let's go in," said Robbin.

"Eh?" said Urgum.

"It'll be fun!" said Ruinn.

"Yeah, we could lay the harp across two tables," said Rekk.

"Then we put the harp player on top," said Rakk.

"And then Robbin could sit on him," said Ruinn. "He'd come out in slices."

"Oh please, Dad, can we go in? *Please?*" said the boys.

"Oh go on, you've talked me into it," smiled Urgum, stepping towards the door.

"No, wait!" said Divina in a panic. "I've just thought of a little job you can do for me instead."

And that's how Urgum and the boys ended up toddling down to the craft market to buy a little blue cardigan for Googoobah. Although it wasn't nearly as good as fighting and waving axes, it was a lot better than slurping cherry water, so they did their best to make the most of it.

"YARGHHH!"

shouted Urgum.

"YARGHHH!"

shouted the savage sons.

"Death to all cardigans!" shouted Urgum, waving his axe madly.

"Death to all cardigans!" shouted the savage sons.

When they got to the knitting stall, they found three very huge and very sad savages standing behind it. Urgum felt desperately sorry for them because, although they had massive muscular bodies, thick powerful foreheads and heavy knuckles, there they were, stuck selling soft woolly ear muffs, socks with toes and little stuffed animals in all the same colours as sick.

"Can I help you, sir?" said one of the knitter boys, trying to pretend that there was nothing unusual around his neck.

"Dad," whispered Rakk. "He's wearing a pink fluffy scarf."

"Shhh!" said Urgum.

"And his mate's wearing a knitted tank top!" sniggered Rekk.

"Leave it," said Urgum. "Poor devils. We won't mention it."

"But it's got a picture of a sheep on it."

The tank-top knitter boy gulped a big gulp. "It's a present from my auntie," he muttered sheepishly.

"I understand," said Urgum, trying to tear his eyes away from the sheep's pom-pom eyes and loose flappy tail. Urgum indicated the third knitter boy standing behind the counter, who was both scarfless and tank-topless. "At least your mate's got away with it."

The third knitter boy bit his lip and blushed. Ruinn had crept round the stall and was peering in from the side. "Dad!" he shouted excitedly. "He's wearing rainbow leg warmers!"

Urgum looked at the three savages, and they looked back at him. What was there to say? They were wearing dodgy knitwear, he was looking through a pile of little woolly cardigans. It was all too embarrassing and needed to end as quickly as possible. A voice came from one of the bags slung over Robbin's shoulder.

"She said get a blue one, Dad," Raymond reminded him.

"That'll be two tannas, please," said Tank Top.

Ruinn passed over two little coins.

"Thank you," said Urgum.

"You're welcome," said Leg Warmers.

Urgum and the boys turned to go back to the Gossiperia. "Yarghhhh," said Urgum, trying to forget the awful unsavageness of the whole event.

"Excuse me?" said Raymond's voice from the bag. "What was that supposed to be?"

"I said yarghhh," said Urgum.

"You *said* yarghhh?" gasped Raymond. "You can't just say yarghhh, you have to shout it! If people start saying yarghhh, it'll be the end of savagery as we know it."

"I can't help it," said Urgum helplessly. "How am I supposed to be savage when I'm buying a little blue cardigan?"

"Oh, for goodness' sake," said Raymond. Out of one of his bags shot a hand, which pointed over Robbin's shoulder at Tank Top. "OI, YOU!" he shouted. "Yes, YOU, the fat one in the girlie jumper, I'm talking to YOU. You've got some nerve charging two tannas for that snot rag."

"Shhh!" said Urgum. "Isn't he suffering enough? Don't embarrass him more."

"Him embarrassed?" said Raymond. "How about ME

embarrassed? My dad and savage brothers have just meekly bought a baby cardigan from three blokes dressed like pixies. I might be chopped up and stuck in these bags, but I'm not standing for this. I'll fight all of you!"

Raymond's bags started thrashing and kicking around so much that Robbin ended up dropping them on the ground. A foot shot out of one and kicked Urgum on the knee.

THOKK!

"Owww," shouted Urgum, clutching his sore leg to his chest and trying to kick Raymond's foot back with the other one. But the foot had already slipped behind him, where it jumped up and hoofed him on the bottom.

WHUMP!

For the first time, the knitter boys actually smiled. A hand flipped itself from another bag, shimmied up Ruinn's vest and tried to pull his nose off.

SKURR-EEK!

"Ho ho!" laughed the knitter boys.

"I hope you're not laughing at my family," said the voice bag, which had landed on the knitting counter next to a stuffed yellow elephant. "You great soft puddle of dandies."

Suddenly Fluffy Scarf pulled a mallet from under the counter and smashed it down, but Raymond's bag rolled away just in time, leaving the yellow elephant to take the full force of the hit. All that elephant had ever wanted was to be packaged up with a set of bath salts and offered as second prize in a raffle, but maybe that was never meant to be. Who knows? Meanwhile a large fat hand closed around Fluffy Scarf's wrist. "That's my little brother in that bag," said Robbin. He jerked the wrist up and round to the side so that the mallet caught Tank Top an absolute peach on the chin.

WABLATT

And thus, with the opening formalities concluded, the fight was under way.

"YARGHHH!"

shouted Urgum, the sons and the knitter boys as they all piled into each other.

"YARGHHH YARGHHH YARGHHH!"

"That's more like it," said Raymond.

BAFF SLOKK DUMPA WHUMPA CRUNCH

It wasn't long before five chunky blue-skinned savages had hurried over from their wives' home-made cake stall to see what the noise was about. They'd been made to wear frilly aprons to keep themselves clean and tidy, so no wonder they were itching for a bit of a joust. "Aw, look!" shouted one of them. "It's a little tiff about baby clothes."

Leg Warmers was just about to bang the twins' heads together, but he decided he'd got time to return a bit of abuse first. "Back off, you flour-faced sugar sprinklers. Go and ice your fairy cakes."

"Good one!" cheered Rekk and Rakk.

"Thanks," said Leg Warmers, before finishing the job in hand.

KADDUNK!

Urgum and the others all looked round hopefully. So far it had been quite a reasonable little scrap but it was just

starting to go a bit stale. The blue cake-stall guys looked like good news, but just like any other well-brought-up savages, they were waiting for a proper invitation to weigh in.

"Hey!" shouted Urgum. "Why don't you go back to sticking cream in your doughnuts? Or are you scared of creasing your little aprons?"

"Oh, that's telling them!" said Tank Top, who had been trying to hack the cardigan out of Urgum's hand with a size-eight crochet hook. Sure enough, it was all the encouragement the blue savages needed. Suddenly it was all in together.

It just got better and better. The pottery dads came over and dived in, breaking flowery plates over everybody's heads, then the frilly-lampshade brigade brought the ornamental candle dippers along to dish out a spanking to the hair-braiding mob. By that time, there was no holding back the lacy-curtain crew, who swapped a few knocks with the squashed fruit barmen and the embroidered-shoulder-bag gang, and soon the only person not fighting was a little man in the middle wearing a green and gold uniform and a hat six sizes too big. Rather crossly he went round gathering up Raymond's bags and tossing them into a pile.

"All right, you, you're under arrest," said the little man.

"Oi!" shouted Raymond's voice bag. "What's going on now?"

"Is that you, Raymond?" The little man looked carefully at the pile of twitching bags full of living body parts. "Sorry, I didn't recognize you."

"Hunjah!" said Raymond crossly. "What's your game?"

"I'm the market-stalls manager," said Hunjah, who happened to be the patheticest barbarian the Lost Desert had ever known. "I'm here to settle disputes about who can have which stall. I saw you start this fight, and thought you were trying to take over the knitting stall."

"Do I LOOK like I want to take over a knitting stall?" demanded Raymond's voice bag.

"No," admitted Hunjah, as a shower of somebody else's teeth clattered into the side of his head. "Sorry, my mistake. It's just that some pretty nasty arguments break out over who can sell what."

"Why would anybody argue about that?" asked Raymond.

"Are you kidding?" said Hunjah. "Everybody wants a stall here! All you've got to do is glue a few old shells to a bottle, then you can sell it to the Laplace softhands for ten silver tannas. It's the easiest way to make money in the Lost Desert. The trouble is that there isn't room for everybody, so the craft makers put all their biggest and meanest relatives in charge of their stalls to make sure nobody pushes them off. Oh, that reminds me…" Hunjah took a sundial out of his pocket and looked at it, then blew a whistle round his neck.

Pweeee

All the savages immediately stopped fighting and looked round. Hunjah held up a ridiculously huge bunch of keys and rattled them. "I'll be closing up soon, so could you all speed it up a bit? I don't want any trouble."

"Fair enough," they all shouted, and then went back to fighting a lot faster. They didn't want to upset the market-stalls manager, even if he was the patheticest barbarian the Lost Desert had ever known.

Thanks to everybody cooperating, they all managed to get their final punches, chops, wallops and kicks in just before closing time, then the savages that could still walk and talk all linked arms and gave a rousing cheer of appreciation to the ones who couldn't. As they drifted away laughing, comparing scars and shouting a few final **YARGHHHS**, Urgum and the others went over to find Raymond. Urgum roared with laughter when he heard what Hunjah's job was.

"Hunjah's in charge of the craft market?" scoffed Urgum. "How sad is that?"

"What are you doing here, anyway?" demanded Hunjah, feeling slightly hurt.

"I had a bit of shopping to do," said Urgum, trying to make it sound tough and savage.

"You? SHOPPING?" gasped Hunjah. "You're supposed to be the fiercest savage the Lost Desert has ever known. It's thanks to you that I get called Hunjah the Headless."

"Let's not go into that," said Urgum.

"No, let's not," said all the other sons, feeling a bit queasy. They knew what was coming.

"It's not my fault," said Hunjah. "You're the bloke who knocked my head off with one punch!" Hunjah grabbed his own ears and lifted his head clear away from

his neck. Holding it high, he looked down on them from under his big hat. Ukky!

"Hang on," said Hunjah's head suspiciously. "We don't sell axes or daggers or anything like that. So what exactly were you shopping for?"

"Er, ah, well…" said Urgum rather embarrassedly. But there was no escaping the gruesome truth. "A little blue knitted cardigan."

Poor Urgum. If there was one thing certain to make him feel awful, it was when a head, which was being held up by the ears and wearing a hat six sizes too big, was feeling sorry for him.

"I thought I had it rough," said Hunjah's head. "But Urgum the Axeman buying a little blue knitted cardigan? How sad is *that*?"

Showdown at the Gossiperia

While Urgum and the boys had thought they were being tough at the craft market, they had missed a far nastier event back at the Gossiperia.

Divina and Glamora had spent an unbelievable amount of time discussing how smart Googoobah would look in the lovely little blue cardigan that Urgum had gone to fetch. Glamora had suggested he might look even handsomer in green, but Divina was convinced blue was the right choice. Even though the conversation drove Molly nuts, she didn't mind. At least her mum was happy, and so was Googoobah. He was on the floor shaking a toy as violently as he could.

ChiSka ChiSka ChiSka

Molly had made it for him out of a rattlesnake's tail glued to an old dagger handle and it was Googoobah's favourite thing in the world, partly because it was so noisy, but mainly because it was his only thing in the world.

ChiSka
ChiSka
ChiSka

Molly felt very proud. This was even better than going to the craft market and then coming back pretending you hadn't had a massive fight. (Molly knew exactly what her dad and the boys would be doing.)

Just then there was a huge blare of trumpets from outside and a thick shower of rose petals were tossed through the door, completely covering the floor. Two slaves came in spraying perfume everywhere and then a third slave followed, leading a giant blindfolded tiger on the end of a golden chain. Reclining on the back of the tiger was a very slim woman with huge red lips, stupidly big earrings and a completely ridiculous hat.

"It's Suprema!" said Divina and Glamora, switching on their biggest, falsest smiles.

The slaves immediately picked up the grandest chair in the place, tipped the three old gentlemen who were sitting on it on to the floor, and positioned it next to their table. Suprema slid off the tiger on to the chair, where she lay with the back of her hand resting on her forehead.

"Dahlings, just don't ask," she said.

"What's the matter?" asked Divina.

"Mum, she said not to ask," said Molly.

"That's not how it works," hissed Divina.

"Don't tell me, I look dreadful, I know," said Suprema, holding a little hand mirror up to her face. "It's the burden of motherhood."

"YOU?" gasped the ladies, staring at Suprema's tummy area, which wasn't easy because she hadn't really got one. "When's it due?"

"Already here, dears," said Suprema. "But don't ask

where it came from. I promised the princess I wouldn't tell that I'd been asked to foster her new baby boy, lest the poor little mite fall into the hands of kidnappers."

"Princess?"

"Shhh! Did I say that? You didn't hear me. My mind is a mess, the stress, the exhaustion. But since the secret's out, you might as well have a peek."

She clicked her fingers and four more slaves came in through the door carrying a golden sedan cot. In attendance behind them walked a selection of nannies, maids, cooks and a troupe of clowns banging tambourines and blowing tooty trumpets.

"MAKE WAY FOR THE DISGUISED BABY PRINCE!" shouted the slaves.

"I know it's wrong of me to risk his life by sneaking him out in this way, but I had to take that chance. I can only hope that no one's noticed him."

Glamora was already on her feet and was staring into the sedan cot. "Is that really the new baby prince?"

"Of course!" snapped Suprema. "The princess delivered him to me herself this morning. She begged me to look after her child. What could I say?"

"LIAR."

Suprema looked like she'd been slapped in the face with an old nappy. Was it Molly or Divina who'd said it? Both were glaring at her with exactly the same face – one eyebrow raised and lips drawn tight. Supressed sniggering came from the slaves, even the tiger was grinning under his blindfold. It was Glamora who broke the silence.

"Suprema, dear," said Glamora. "You didn't really see the princess, did you? Everyone knows she's so beautiful you'd be blinded."

"Oh, well, if you're going to be pedantic!" snapped Suprema. "No, it wasn't exactly the princess, it was the Mistress of the Royal Bedchamber. Apparently the palace isn't safe any more, so she brought the prince round to me and made me swear that no one would ever know."

"You should have kept him at home, then," said Molly, who was giving the tiger a friendly stroke.

Suprema shot her a filthy look. "Is that fair? Is that really fair? Would you condemn this poor little mite to a lifetime trapped within four walls, never to see one golden ray of sunlight, never to hear the happy chatter of the townsfolk, never to see the majestic spectacle of me choosing a new hat? If I'd kept him inside one moment longer, he would have lost the will to live. I had to bring him out even if it risked us being seen."

"So how long was he forced to stay inside?"

"He had to wait until I had my make-up on." Suprema treated herself to another look in her mirror.

"That's not very long," exclaimed Molly.

"Oh yes it is," muttered Divina. "I'm surprised that baby hasn't had time to grow a beard."

Glamora's eyes darted between Divina and Suprema. She loved it when things got catty. "Divina's been left with a new baby too," she said, to stir things up a bit.

"Oh, is that what that thing is?" said Suprema, noticing Googoobah for the first time.

"It's not a thing," said Molly. "It's Googoobah."

Googoobah introduced himself with a little burp and wave of his rattle.

Chiska Chiska Chiska

"Whatever," said Suprema. "It's certainly not a prince. Rags, dribble – yuk! Don't let it near me."

Divina's eyes narrowed to tiny slits and Molly hissed, but it was Googoobah who came up with the cleverest retort. He gave his toy an extra hard shake.

Chiska Chiska Chissssska...PLOMP!

The rattle flew over and buried itself in Suprema's hat.

"Argh! That could have killed me!" Suprema shrieked so loudly that she set off a barrage of frightened screams from the golden sedan cot. "Now see what you've done," she shouted accusingly. A nanny immediately picked the baby up while a maid hurriedly retrieved Googoobah's rattle and waved it in the baby's face. Almost immediately the screams died away.

"Could we have that back?" asked Divina.

"That's our property now," said Suprema. "Your thing gave it to the prince."

"But that's his only toy," said Molly.

"It *was* his only toy," said Suprema.

Molly's heart sunk. She could always make another, but it wouldn't be the same and Googoobah would know it. He was already starting to make sad little whimpery noises.

"Oh, shut it up, for goodness' sake!" said Suprema. "Honestly, Divina, why do you ever pretend that you can raise children properly? What can you give them? *Nothing!*"

Oooh! That was an unforgivable thing to say and they all knew it. Glamora took a dainty slurp of cherry water, but secretly she was running all over the walls and ceiling and whooping in excitement.

"I can raise children better than you," said Divina as quietly as a butterfly burns in a candle flame.

"Hardly!" retorted Suprema. "What do you think, Glamora? Which of us can raise a child better?"

"I don't know," said Glamora. "But I do know how we can find out."

Glamora pulled a copy of *Modern Savage* magazine from her

bag. It was neat pile of dried skins covered with writing and pictures and full of suggestions of what to do when you've got far too much time and money to waste. She opened it up and showed them an advert for something calling itself THE GRAND BABY GALA!

"They hold it every year," said Glamora. "There's a prize for the bonniest baby. All you need to do is enter your babies and see who does best."

"Your thing will never win!" sniffed Suprema. "I mean, look at it in those dirty old rags."

"Those old rags are *not* dirty," retorted Divina coldly. "And besides, Urgum and the boys have gone to buy him a super new cardigan. He'll look stunning."

"Here's Dad now," said Molly.

For a moment Divina's sweet smile returned. She was confident that Googoobah in his smart blue cardigan would wipe that smug smirk off Suprema's face. But then she saw Urgum and the boys stumbling in with clothes ripped, blood dripping, bashed noses, ripped out hair, and all of them with stupid satisfied grins. Divina was still doing the exact same sweet smile, but her left eyebrow had switched to the "kill kill kill" position. The sons immediately dived behind their father for safety.

"So did you get the cardigan, Dad?" asked Molly.

"Eh?" said Urgum. Divina's smile was starting to make his eyes hurt. "Oh, yes, of course." He held out his closed fist. A raw knuckle bone poked through a patch of torn skin. "I think it might have got very slightly marked along the way," admitted Urgum. "But not so you'd really notice."

Slowly he opened his thick fingers. Inside was a squished-up squelchy red blob. Molly picked it up with her fingertips and opened it out. One sleeve was almost ripped away, a bite had been taken out of the collar, the ribbons were torn to shreds and the whole thing was glued up with thick blood. It's just a shame there was one tiny bit of blue wool still showing, otherwise Urgum could have pretended he'd accidentally brought home a handful of lizard guts.

Divina could have screamed. Divina should have screamed. In fact Divina was desperate to scream, but

(a) LIZARD GUTS

(b) CARDIGAN

wouldn't Suprema have just *loved* that? So would Glamora, for that matter, but Divina had no intention of giving either of them the satisfaction. Instead Divina coolly took the little bloody rag and tried it on Googoobah who immediately started sucking the dripping sleeve.

"There, Glamora, dear," she said with her same sweet smile. "I told you. Blue is definitely his colour."

TiNKa-CHiNKLE

They all turned to see that Suprema's earrings had both fallen to the floor and smashed. Her face was frozen in solid horror.

"No sense of fashion, some people," said Urgum, grinning fondly at Googoobah. All the nannies, maids, slaves, cooks, clowns, Molly, Glamora, the sons, the three old gentlemen that had been tipped off the chair and the tiger cheered in agreement. As for Divina, she had been so so so *so* cross with Urgum that at first she didn't realize she was laughing her head off.

Although Urgum didn't always do exactly what she wanted, Divina couldn't complain this time. After all, he had absolutely and completely wiped that smug smirk off Suprema's face. Sometimes being married to him was really utterly brilliant.

Just a Bit of Fun

Urgum was sitting on a rock outside his cave, moodily sharpening his axe with a grindstone. It was the day before the baby competition and somehow it didn't seem worth the effort. Picking a fight with some bored craft traders had been easy enough, but even Urgum couldn't see how he'd manage to get a decent scrap going with a load of soppy mums parading their washed and poshed infants around.

"What's up with you?" asked Mungoid, striding over and parking himself down.

"Divina's making us all go to this baby gala," said Urgum. "You don't fancy coming along too, do you?"

"Sorry, I can't!" said Mungoid. "I've got better things to do. Mind you, it could get pretty vicious."

"This is no time for jokes!" snapped Urgum. "I'm supposed to be the fiercest savage the Lost Desert has ever known. I should be standing knee-deep in blood and gore waving my axe, not plodding round with a bag full of nappies and bottles and chatting about how to knit booties."

"Oh, so you've not heard about this kidnapping plot, then?"

"What's that got to do with anything?" said Urgum. "That's softhand stuff. They grab somebody and ask for money. It's no good grabbing any of us, we haven't got any."

"But this is to kidnap the prince! Maybe they want to force the royal family to leave or something."

"Do I look like royal family to you?" said Urgum. "Fat chance of me getting any action."

"Well, it doesn't need a kidnapping for a bonny baby competition to get nasty," said Mungoid. "I went to one once. They called it the Rattle Battle. I was one of the judge's bodyguards."

"The judge needs bodyguards?" Urgum sat up excitedly. "That's brilliant, but why?"

"Because the judge has to tell one mum that her kid is the bonniest."

"So?"

"So that's the same as telling all the other mums that their kids are uglier. Did you ever tell Divina how ugly Ruinn was?"

"Are you kidding?" said Urgum. "She'd have ripped my lips off."

"That's why the judge needs bodyguards," said Mungoid. "Imagine what it would be like to upset a whole army of Divinas."

"Oo-er!" said Urgum.

Inside the cave, Googoobah was sitting up watching Divina with great interest. She had spent ages bent over a tub of soapy water with her sleeves rolled up, frantically pummelling away at something under the bubbles. Eventually she pulled out a short piece of ribbon and stared at it closely.

"What do you think, Molly?" she asked.

"It looks fine," said Molly, who was standing beside her holding the rest of the little blue cardigan.

"You're not looking properly," said Divina. "Maybe just one more little scrub…"

"Mum!" said Molly. "It's only a little ribbon to go on a little cardigan to go on a little baby. He doesn't care what it looks like, do you, Googoobah?"

Googoobah grinned and pulled his new toy out of his mouth and gave it a friendly wave. Sadly, this toy didn't make any noise, but a squeak did come from one of Raymond's bags in the corner.

"Stoppit!" giggled Raymond. "The air rushing through the hole makes me go all shivery."

"Don't wave it around," Molly said to Googoobah. "After all, it was very kind of Raymond to lend you one of his ears."

Googoobah obediently put the ear back in his mouth and sucked it again.

"See?" said Molly. "He's

happy enough, so give it a rest, Mum."

"But the gala is tomorrow," said Divina, as if Molly could have forgotten. "I just want him to look like somebody's made a bit of an effort."

A *bit* of an effort? Molly sighed. Ever since they'd got home from the Gossiperia, Divina had been going at Googoobah like a mad thing. He'd been bathed, oiled and perfumed, his tiny little hairs had been tried out in dozens of different styles, and most importantly, every strand of his new cardigan had been dismantled, scrubbed, re-wound and pieced back together. While all this had been going on, the boys had barely dared come out of their room, Urgum had kept well out of the way outside and Molly had tiptoed round, doing her best to keep Googoobah quiet.

"I'll be honest with you, Mum," said Molly. "I wish Glamora had never mentioned this bonniest baby prize."

"Why?" said Divina. "It's just a bit of fun with Suprema. After all, she is one of my oldest friends."

"Then why can't you just let her win?"

"Because I hate her."

"But what happens if she beats you?"

Divina froze in position, gripping the edge of the wash tub so hard her knuckles went white. Finally she took a deep breath and held the ribbon to her face again. She stared at it, saw an imaginary speck of something on it, and once again plunged it into the soapy water.

Molly had had enough, so she went outside to find that Urgum had given up sharpening his axe. Instead he was challenging Mungoid to a "who-can-pull-their-bottom-lip-out-the-furthest?" contest.

"Dad," said Molly. "You know that Mum HAS to win the bonniest baby prize?"

"Isn't she a bit old?" asked Urgum, still pulling his lip out.

"Nonsense," said Mungoid. "I bet she'd look dead cute in a nappy and little woolly knitted booties."

Urgum thought this was so funny that he had to yank his bottom lip right up over his nose to make absolutely sure that no great laugh could shoot out into the cave and land in Divina's ear. Mungoid blushed furiously. "I'm so sorry," he muttered. "That was supposed to be a secret thinking thing, not a say-out-loud thing."

"Yes, well, the point is," said Molly, trying not to think of Divina in a nappy, "what will Mum be like if she comes home and Gubbs has lost out to Suprema's baby prince?"

"That can't happen," said Urgum. "Gubbs is the tops."

"I know, but it won't help," said Molly. "Suprema always bribes judges."

"Oh does she really?" said Urgum. "Then I better have a quiet word with this judge."

"What will you say, Dad?"

"I'll say that it doesn't matter how much money somebody might give him, he can't spend it if he's dead."

Mungoid nodded. "That sounds fair. But, Urgum, what will you do about the judge's bodyguards?"

"Now *there's* a good reason to sharpen my axe," grinned Urgum, and he picked up his grindstone again.

All Stood Up

On the next day, Mungoid was starting to wish he'd gone to the baby gala after all. Instead he was sitting in the Parad-Ice Cream Parlour looking very fed up. In front of him was a soggy green blob on a plate which he hadn't started, partly because he hated ice cream but mainly because of good manners. In front of the empty seat beside him was a very huge mass of shiny wet colour that had been the house special when he'd first ordered it, but had since melted into a sticky goo. He sighed and looked out of the window again. Of course he'd expected Grizelda to be a bit late, that's what really classy girls are like, he told himself. And let's face it, he'd hadn't been waiting *all* afternoon. Well, not yet anyway. Of course, he'd already waited all morning, but that didn't count because they hadn't arranged to meet until lunchtime.

Lots of strange and interesting people had been in and out since he'd arrived, but he didn't give any of them much thought until suddenly the door crashed open and three small hairy savages barged their way in. Their hair was short and spiky, revealing their grey craggy faces, and they wore thick leather work tunics. They clambered on to stools and banged their table impatiently to bring the waiter running over. All three shouted at him at once, but he hadn't a clue what they were saying, so they ordered by pointing at what other people were having.

Despite being fed up, Mungoid was curious, especially when their order arrived. All three immediately tipped their ice creams on the floor and started taking bites from the fancy plates instead. For a while they crunched away in silence and just stared round at the other customers suspiciously. Mungoid looked down at the jagged edge of his own plate where he'd taken a nibble. For some reason he hadn't quite worked out yet, he decided to rest his great hand over his bite marks so that the small savages wouldn't notice. Eventually they relaxed and put their heads together to discuss

something terribly secret, but it was obvious from the way they kept saying "eh?" at each other that they were all fairly deaf. It wasn't long before their voices were back to full volume, confident that nobody else in the place could understand them. Unfortunately for them, they had no way of knowing that the huge hulking savage poking a lonely cherry round a plate of green slop with the end of his finger was a very distant cousin. Mungoid had recognized them as being three troggyls because, just like them, he was also descended from the very rocks of the Lost Desert. And that's why, just like the troggyls, he couldn't resist chomping through a bit of baked clay plate every now and then.

Mungoid couldn't understand exactly what they were saying, but then neither could they because even though they'd raised their voices, they were still shouting "eh?" at each other. However, he did recognize the terms for "chief", "grab", "winner", "must", "infant", and "I beg your pardon, would you mind repeating that", although the last one was easy because it was just "eh?"

Long after the noisy troggyls had gone, Mungoid was still thinking it over. Chief grab winner must infant? He tried mixing the words up. Grab must winner infant chief? Winner infant must chief grab… that was it! The winner infant must be the chief, grab him.

Mungoid slapped his head – it was the kidnap plot! "Winner infant" must refer to the winner of the baby gala. The troggyls had reckoned that the winner must be the "chief" – in other words the prince – and they intended to grab him! If Googoobah won and then got kidnapped, what would Divina be like? Mungoid had to warn Urgum immediately.

"Hi, Mungoid," said Grizelda, who had just walked in. "GET OUT OF MY WAY!" Mungoid leapt up but his foot slipped on the troggyls' pool of ice cream on the floor and he landed face first in Grizelda's giant house special.

SKRUNCH-A-PLOP

Too dazed to move, he was drowning in peach and pineapple sauce until the waiter rushed over and hauled his face out of the bowl. Mungoid was just about to open his eyes when he heard Grizelda mutter, "Oh lordy! Do you think he needs the kiss of life?"

Mungoid immediately cancelled his eye-opening plan and lolled his head a bit.

"Oh, dear, I think he might," said the waiter.

WOW! Mungoid slumped backwards, pretending that

he was tottering on the brink of death.

"You hold his head up and I'll try to put my mouth on his."

Mungoid instantly made a full recovery. Grizelda holding his head was really nice, but seeing the waiter's face bending towards him hadn't been quite so good.

"Sorry I'm late, Mungoid," said Grizelda.

"That's fine!" said Mungoid. "Just got here myself, actually."

"But I thought you were leaving?"

"Really?" Mungoid tried to remember why he'd jumped up. There had definitely been a good reason, but it was all a bit confusing, especially as Grizelda was mopping his face while the waiter fussed around, clearing the messy table and inviting them to sit.

"Sorry about the floor," said the waiter. "Will you accept a couple of free specials, courtesy of the management?"

"That'll do for me," said Grizelda, licking her lips. "But did you want something too, Mungoid?"

Mungoid thought about it. He was sitting at a table with Grizelda. Just the two of them. There was absolutely nothing else in the whole of the Lost Desert that the dear old ugly Ungoid could possibly have wanted.

Toes and an Hourglass

The Grand Baby Gala was being held in Dream Valley, which cut through the outer gardens of Laplace Palace. At the top of the steps leading down into the valley were two majestic entrances, each with a big flag fluttering overhead, one in blue and the other in pink.

Urgum and the others joined the crowd, making their way towards the blue flag when they heard the unmistakable sound of clowns blowing tooty trumpets from the pink entrance. Glamora suddenly appeared by their side.

"You're here at last!" she said. "Suprema's already going in."

"We guessed that," said Molly.

"Ha!" said Divina, who was proudly cradling Googoobah in his immaculately clean cardigan. "Then she can't have had time to wash him properly. Or change him. Or dress him. Or something. Ha!"

There was a bit of a commotion going on at the front of the pink queue. Suprema was on her tiger screeching at her nannies. "You fools! It's pink for girls. The prince must go in the blue entrance!" Suprema then looked round at the crowd and clapped her hand over her mouth. "Oops, sorry, did I say *prince?*" She gave a naughty giggle. "I meant *perfectly normal boring little baby*, just like all yours are."

"I bet she told her nannies to go in the wrong way on purpose," said Molly. "Just so she could shout about the prince."

"I don't fancy his chances much if there really are kidnappers about," said Urgum.

They had all thought that the bonniest baby competition would just be a single line-up of mums and babies waiting for the judge to walk past, but oh no. When *Modern Savage* magazine ran an event, it didn't mess about. As they made their way down the grand marble stairs to the gardens at the bottom of the valley, they saw the main stage with a banner reading "Bonniest Baby", but there was nobody near it. Instead the crowds were all gathered around several smaller areas where other events were happening.

They passed a sign saying "Top Toes" and Molly saw a bunch of mums all pulling the little woolly socks and booties from their babies' feet.

"Do they really have a competiton for the nicest baby's toes?" asked Molly.

"Not the *nicest*," said Glamora, studying the rules in her copy of *Modern Savage*. "The most."

"The *most*?" said Molly.

The twins immediately turned on each other. "I could win that," said Rekk. "I've got loads of toes."

"I've got more than you!" said Rakk.

BIFFBAM WOPBANG WALLOP

One proud mum was holding up a particularly wide little sock while an official with special magnifying glasses was staring at her charming little girl's foot. As he worked along the toes he recited: "This little piggy went to market. This little piggy stayed home. This little piggy had roast beef and this little piggy had roast beef too but this little piggy didn't like beef, so he had sausages. This little piggy fell in the mud. This little piggy could wiggle his ears. This little piggy went wee wee wee all the way home. This little piggy kept his pants dry. This little piggy…"

They couldn't wait for all the piggies, so they moved on. "The bonniest baby event is last," said Glamora.

"Good," said Urgum. "Because there's somebody I want to have a quiet word with. Come on, boys, we'll catch up with the ladies later."

Urgum and the sons strode off purposefully through the crowd towards the official's tent. Glamora's eyes glittered excitedly. "Is he going to have a big fight like he did at the craft market?"

Divina gave her an odd look. "You call that a big fight? You've seen nothing yet."

"Ooooh!" twittered Glamora.

The baby gala was full of the most unexpected things, and one of Molly's favourites was the giant hourglass. Almost all the sand had got down to the bottom, but there was still one last bit left to trickle through the hole. Standing around the hourglass was an anxious crowd of extremely lumpy-looking ladies and nervous men. Nearby was a row of tents with midwives running in and out fetching towels and bowls of warm water, while a merry chorus of wails, moans and screams came from inside. Suddenly one tent flap was pushed aside and a proud new father rushed out carrying a tiny yowking bundle, which he immediately thrust in the face of an official.

"Not too late, are we?" said the father.

The official looked at the sand left in the top of the hourglass. "No, not quite. Well done, you're the winner!" The crowd gave a frustrated moan but were interrupted when another new father shot out from a different tent clutching another baby. The official raised an eyebrow. "Ooops, no, sorry. This one's in the lead now."

The crowd moaned again, and some of the ladies even started jumping up and down to try to hurry things on a bit.

"What's going on with them?" asked Molly.

Glamora checked her programme. "It's the Youngest Baby Award. The last baby to be born before the sand runs out wins."

The latest father was staring at the sand, which was taking for ever to trickle away. "Come on, come on," he said. Funnily enough, all the other fathers-to-be had their heads down by the big bumps and were shouting to the person inside "Come on, come on" too.

"They haven't got much time left," said Molly, looking at the sand. "How long does it take for a baby to come out, Mum?"

"That depends on the baby," said Divina. "Robbin took days because he was a bit embarrassed about coming out without any clothes on, but the twins had a race to be first so they were very quick."

Suddenly the most terrible ear-splitting high-pitched chord of shrieks came from behind them.

WARR-EEEEEEE!

Clasping their ears, they all turned round to see the Loudest Yowk competition was under way. A row of babies had been strapped into highchairs, and then a long plank had been laid in front of them. Fastened on the plank in front of each baby was an irresistible bowl of syrup slugs, but just as the babies had been halfway through helping themselves, two slaves wearing thick ear protection had yanked the plank away. The officials standing right over at the far end of the gardens were listening attentively and making notes as the tots registered their objections, but it all got a bit complicated.

The sudden barrage of yowk had shocked the lumpy ladies so much that it gave them the extra boost they

needed, and almost all of them waddled hurriedly into the tents. The Yowk judges were having trouble separating the baby yowks from the new mummy noises, which led to a rather unexpected result. The prize for the Youngest Baby went to three fat triplets, while everybody agreed that the Loudest Yowk award should go to their mother.

A Quiet Word

U rgum and the boys found the officials' tent, which was full of officials having official drinks and official conversation and telling official jokes. Yawn. But luckily it was being guarded by lots of far more exciting people, who made some promising **GRRRR** noises as Urgum approached. Their leader had a gleaming metal badge pinned to his chest, which was pretty cool because he was only wearing trousers. "What do you lot want?" he snarled.

"I need to have a quiet word with one of the judges," said Urgum.

"Tough," smirked the leader, giving Urgum a poke in

the tummy. "You're not walking in past us."

"We've no intention of walking in past you," said Urgum. Behind him the boys all grinned and pulled out their daggers, clubs, mallets and maces. "We're going to walk in *over* you."

YARGHHHHH!

By the time Urgum and the boys had got inside, the officials were all backed against the far wall and having an official scream.

"OH GROW UP!" shouted Urgum, wiping a bit of blood off his axe. For a while everything fell silent. "I just want a quiet word with one of you."

"Which one?" muttered the nearest official.

"The one judging the bonniest baby," said Urgum.

"If you want to bribe him, you're wasting your time."

"Do I look like I'm coming to bribe anyone? All I want is to make sure the result is fair. So which one of you is it?"

The officials all tried to sneak outside but it was too late. The biggest son, Robbin, was blocking the way and smiling politely. "I'm sorry, but could we just keep you for a moment longer?" He had lovely manners, did Robbin. Mind you, he also had a huge spiked club which had fresh bits of bodyguard body dangling off it.

Urgum dragged a table into the middle of the floor and then got the twins to climb up on to it. They both waved their daggers and the officals all cowered back in fear.

"Right, we'll try again," said Urgum. "Which one of you is it? Either you tell me or I'll set my toughest son on you."

"Yeah, and that's me!" said Rekk.

"You?" snorted Rakk. "You couldn't fight a bubble."

"Who says?"

"Me!"

WAM
BAK
ZOKKA
SLASH

Once again the officials screamed in horror as the

savage twins laid into each other.

"THERE," shouted Urgum over the noise. "That's what they're prepared to do to each other. So think what they'd do to YOU!"

Still screaming, every official in the room immediately turned and pointed to one man sitting huddled in the corner.

"So that's him," said Urgum. "OK, boys, take this lot out and keep them out." Robbin stepped aside, and the officials all dashed away over the groaning bodyguards with the boys following them. Once Urgum was alone with the judge, he walked over and waved his bloodstained axe in a friendly way.

"I want a quiet word with you," said Urgum.

"Whatever," said the man forlornly without looking up. Urgum realized this would have been quite a big fellow if he got to his feet and put his shoulders back, but hunched over on a small chair he looked pathetic.

"About this judging," said Urgum. "I do hope you're going to be fair."

"Whatever."

"Because if you've been bribed, I'll hack you into so many bits that your friends will have to suck you up through a straw." For a moment the judge looked up with a strange gleam of hope in his eyes. Urgum was a bit disconcerted so he did another **GRRRR**, then he continued.

"Luckily for you, I can tell you who the winner should be. It's the little lad with the smart blue knitted cardigan. If you pick anybody else I'll know you've been bribed and that wouldn't be fair, would it?"

The judge sighed and looked down again. "Whatever."

When Urgum finally left the tent to find the boys, he was looking very confused.

"So did you have a quiet word with him then, Dad?" asked Ruinn.

"Sort of," said Urgum. He held up his axe and stared at the blade moodily. "It's just that he did it better than me."

"Did what?"

"He had a quiet word," said Urgum. "Just the one word and he said it quietly."

"What word was that?"

Urgum shook his head in despair. "Whatever."

Pewwilezz Dainda

Up in the Halls of Sirrus, Tangor and Tangal were dozing in front of the fire, deliberately taking no interest in the baby gala. Why should they? It was hardly likely to involve any gruesome fights to the death or glorious acts of immensely dangerous stupidity, so there wasn't much for two barbarian gods to get excited about. Besides, the baby was doing fine, and as long as Olk wouldn't let anybody get home without him, Urgum and the others were bound to make sure he stayed safe.

Fplip fplop

It took them a moment to recognize the sound of two large bird feet landing on the cloud outside. They got to the door just in time to see the stork let the nappy fall open and three great shapes come lumbering towards them.

"What do you want?" Tangal called out.

"Urgum and Divina have taken good care of the baby," added Tangor. "So you needn't come in."

It was no good. First the huge Booty Bot squeezed his way in through the door, then did an unexpected roll and ended up knocking Tangor to the floor and sitting on his stomach. Daisybelle tottered in behind him and went to poke her fingers in the fire.

"No no, you mustn't do that," said Tangal, dashing over to pull her hand back. "Fire is hot. Fire is naughty. Fire will burn you. You'll get hurt, and then who's a silly girl?"

Daisybelle angrily snatched her hand free, giving Tangal a nasty scratch on the arm for good measure, then went to poke the fire again. By this time Wedge was in the doorway watching them with his big uncaring blue eyes while his dummy writhed around in his mouth.

"What ... do ... you ... want?" gasped Tangor. Above him Booty Bot swayed from side to side and the heavy nappy squelched ominously.

"AAARGHHHHH!"

screamed Daisybelle, pulling her hand away and scattering hot coals across the room.

"AAARGHHHHH!"

Tangal clasped her hands to her ears and looked at Wedge. "Why are you doing this to us? Why can't you leave us alone?"

"Now then," said Wedge, removing his dummy and dribbling down his "I'm The Boss" bib. "That's not very hospitable, is it? Especially when we've come to do you a favour."

"We don't need … favours," wheezed Tangor. "We are the mighty barbarian gods…"

Wedge gave Booty Bot a nod. The huge baby immediately clouted the mightiness out of the barbarian god by bouncing his bottom up and down on Tangor's guts. Wedge continued. "We just dropped by to let you know that Urgum's baby is in perilous danger."

"Perilous danger?" said Tangal.

"Pewwi-lezz dain-da?" repeated Daisybelle.

"She talks!" exclaimed Tangal.

"Yeah, she's coming on isn't she?" said Wedge. "You'll be glad to know she's about finished teething too."

"What danger?" gasped Tangor.

"Dain-da," repeated Daisybelle.

"This bonniest baby prize, there's a plot to kidnap the winner."

"A plot to kidnap the winner?" said Tangal.

"Oh, don't you start repeating things," said Wedge. "It's bad enough Daisybelle doing it."

"Daybell doon id," grinned Daisybelle.

"How, when, why?" said Tangal.

"I dunno," said Wedge. "That's your problem. But I can tell you one thing – if that baby comes to any harm it'll be all your fault, and you'll get all the blame."

"Why us?"

Wedge raised his eyes to the ceiling. How many times did he have to explain this?

"Because ... You Don't Matter."

Under Starters Orders

At last the main competiton was getting under way. A few officials were fussing around on the big stage arranging a table with a box of prizes which included a large golden nappy, a large silver nappy and two little woolly animals that had mysteriously appeared. Luckily the officials were being far too busy to hear what the animals were saying.

"This is ridiculous!" moaned the pink sheep. "I'm supposed to be an all-powerful ancient deity."

"Oh shut up, Tangor," said the green giraffe. "These are the perfect disguises so we can see exactly what's going on. Remember, if Googoobah wins and there really is a kidnap plot, we could end up baby-minding for eternity."

Down on the ground a crowd of proud mums were standing by the steps, gooing and chirping at their babies as they waited to go up. Even Suprema was holding her own baby. Of course her nose was wrinkled in disgust at the thought of having to carry somebody else's bottom, but she still managed to look terribly smug.

"She's bribed the judge, I know it!" said Glamora.

"It won't do her much good," said Molly. "Not if Dad's had a quiet word with him."

"But what if he never got to see the judge?" asked Glamora.

Just then a ragged team of bodyguards came limping along the path from the official's tent. They were leaning on each other's shoulders for support, some were bandaged and one had a raw bloody patch on his chest where his gleaming metal badge had been.

"Trust me," said Molly. "Dad got to him."

A round of applause broke out in the crowd as a very elegant lady stepped up on to the stage. She had

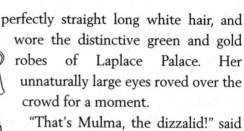

perfectly straight long white hair, and wore the distinctive green and gold robes of Laplace Palace. Her unnaturally large eyes roved over the crowd for a moment.

"That's Mulma, the dizzalid!" said Molly excitedly. "Half woman, half lizard."

"She gives me the creeps," said Glamora.

"I think she's brilliant," said Molly.

The dizzalid's black tongue flickered across her lips before she spoke in her low powerful voice. "Ladies and gentlemen, thank you for joining us in Dream Valley. We are delighted to present the highlight of our afternoon, the bonniest baby competiton. First of all, could I ask the contestants to come up and join me on the stage."

The crowd moved forward. Molly tugged Divina's sleeve. "Good luck, Mum!" she said. "And good luck Googoobah!"

Divina bit her lip and set off. Of course Suprema had managed to be the first person to the steps, but she was taking ages getting up them. Everybody behind her was starting to giggle. Suprema had never had to walk up steps before in her life, and she'd certainly never carried anything heavier than her own hair. When she had almost reached the top, she paused for breath and took the chance to look down and sneer at the others.

"You fools! You're wasting your time. We all know who's the winner here."

The dizzalid came across to find out what was holding everybody up. When she saw Suprema struggling away, almost dropping the baby and catching her dress in her impossibly silly shoes, the dizzalid just looked away and pretended to check the claws on the ends of her thick fingers. Suddenly Suprema shot up the last step and tottered on to the stage. Her eyes nearly burst from her head in fury and she swung round to see exactly WHO had been insolent enough to give her a great big shove on the bottom. But everybody else was still down on the ground well out of reach. Suprema had absolutely no idea what had happened, but whatever it was, it had caused the whole crowd to cheer with laughter. All Suprema could do was walk past the dizzalid who gave her a sweet smile, while secretly tucking her long powerful tail back under her dress.

Soon all the other mums and babies were crowded on to the stage and the dizzalid had moved over to the side nearest to where the bodyguards were standing.

"And now, ladies and gentlemen, it's time to present to you our mystery guest judge. I'm sure he needs no introduction…"

As she said this, the bodyguards all stepped aside to reveal the person they'd been escorting. The dizzalid was right. This judge needed no introduction. A huge disappointed groan came up from the stage. One by one the mothers stomped back down the steps, hissing and cursing.

"What's the matter with them all?" gasped Urgum. "I know Suprema hasn't bribed him."

"She didn't need to," said Glamora. "That's her husband."

"Oh," said Urgum. "Oh dear."

Eventually there was only Divina and Suprema left on the stage. Divina's face was set in stone but Molly knew she'd be fighting back the tears. It was so unfair. Finally, and with her head held high, Divina turned to leave with the others.

"MUM! You stay right where you are!" Ruinn had drawn his gutting knife. "Come on, boys, we need to speak to this judge."

They all pulled their meanest faces and the crowd quickly parted in front of them but Urgum held them back. "Leave it, lads," he said sadly. "I told him I'd chop him up and he just smiled. There's nothing you could do to that poor bloke that would be worse than being married to *her*. It'll take a miracle for Gubbs to win now."

But that's when a huge shadow crossed the stage and a miracle unexpectedly arrived.

Special Delivery

Ruff was dead. He had to be. He couldn't see, he couldn't move, in fact, the only thing he could do was sniff and he didn't want to do that because the smell was utterly revolting. He was being squeezed head-first down a tight tube along with lots of sloppy stuff that boilped and gurgled around him.

It was obvious what had happened. After all his days of flying around, he'd fallen into such a deep sleep that he hadn't noticed the peligantuan landing, tipping its head back and swallowing him. *That's it then*, he thought. The end of Ruff. He started to think about all the people who loved him and who would cry because he'd gone, and who'd miss all the funny little things he used to do. But actually he couldn't think of any so he gave up.

Suddenly he felt himself sliding free of the tube. His face was still gunged up with slime but he could feel a dazzling light all around him and he was flying! Flying? No, to be accurate, he wasn't flying, he was falling. And falling. And falling…

SKAA-PLOPP-A-KORRUNCH!

He had landed on something lumpy, which collapsed beneath him. OUCH! Funny, he'd always imagined when you were dead you landed on nice soft clouds, and he definitely was dead because he could hear a huge crowd cheering as if they were actually pleased to see him. That had never happened when he was alive. As he struggled to his feet the cheering got even louder. Wow, being dead was great! He quickly reached up to wipe the gunk out of his eyes and see what else was waiting for him in the afterlife.

He wasn't sure quite what to expect, but it certainly hadn't included a baby wearing an extemely clean blue woolly cardigan and sucking a severed ear.

The Judge and the Nursemaid

The dizzalid blinked her two eyes separately. She had just been about to formally introduce the judge when a massive black and white slimy lump had fallen from the sky and splattered him right through the floor of the stage. Slowly the lump rose up into a human shape, then stood there scraping the worst of the mess off itself and gawping at the nearest baby in dumbfounded amazement.

The crowd all whooped and cheered and pointed at the intruder, shouting, "Mystery guest judge! Mystery

guest judge!" The dizzalid thought about it. She didn't care who the judge was, or even that he'd just fallen out of a giant bird's bottom. Why not him? Next to her, Suprema was screaming down at the new hole in the stage.

"GET BACK UP HERE! GET UP YOU FOOL!"

But the only answer she got was a manic laugh from her husband.

"HA HAHA HA"

"He can't get up," said one of the bodyguards. "He's been squashed into porridge."

"Then put him in a bucket and bring him up here," ordered Suprema.

"Oh no you don't!" came her husband's voice from the hole. "I like it here. I'm staying."

Suprema was canny enough to know when it was time to change her approach. Suddenly she started gushing, full of concern. "But surely it hurts my poor dahling dearest!"

"It's only a bit of extreme agony. It's better than taking orders from you, so what are you going to do about that? HA HA HA!"

"Ladies and gentlemen!" The dizzalid's low voice bullied its way through the crowd, reducing them all to silence. Her black tongue flickered while one eye stared at Ruff and the other darted between Divina and Suprema. "If we can continue with NO further interruptions, I shall now introduce our mystery guest judge." She gave Ruff a meaningful look.

"Me? A judge? Wow!" Ruff was still feeling groggy and was sure he was dead, but he couldn't care. He had a crowd to play with! He gave them a little wave and a huge cheer came back at him.

"Well, HELLO!" he called out.

Huge cheer.

"It's GOOD to be here!"

Huger cheer.

"So HOW y'all DOIN'?"

Even huger cheer.

"C'mon! Scream if you LOVE me."

Extemely huge stone-dead silence.

Ruff was a bit miffed to discover that he was alive after all, and he was even more miffed when a little

BURP!

came from behind him. He turned to see Divina holding Googoobah.

"Oh, Mum, you've not still got that thing, have you?" he said crossly.

"He is not a thing," hissed Divina. "He is a lovely little boy and this is a bonny baby competition. And you are the judge of this bonny baby competition."

"I know," said Ruff pompously. "So I must be both wise and fair."

"Of course you must be fair, dear," said Divina through gritted teeth. "And it would be very wise of you to be especially fair to your mother."

"What? Even though that thing keeps making me look like a complete plop?"

"Don't blame him. You're the one that just fell out of the back of a bird."

The crowd were getting restless and the dizzalid clearly wanted to get things moving. Ruff looked from Divina to Suprema and back again. "Are there just the two of them?" he asked.

"And one more," came a shrill voice from the crowd. "Coo-ee! Sorry I'm late."

Everybody gasped as a third entry arrived on the stage. Lovely golden curls, bright twinkly eyes, immaculate little dress, super-dooper gloves and booties, freshly washed and spotless bib … even Suprema was taken aback by the appearance of this unexpected challenge. There was only one thing that could possibly stop this otherwise perfect example of bonny babiness winning. She was eighty-seven years old.

"I've always said, if at first you don't succeed…" she chirped as she skipped over to Ruff, "…try, try again!"

The crowd were giggling and the dizzalid was starting to get tetchy. "Get on with it before this whole thing turns into a farce," she hissed. Ruff marched over importantly to inspect the little face that Suprema was presenting to him.

"Rather a lot of make-up, hasn't she?" said Ruff.

"HE!" snapped Suprema. "It's just the odd touch to bring forth his exquisite natural features. You wouldn't know it, but I'm wearing a tiny bit myself." Suprema fluttered her eyelashes at him, which were so long they slapped him on the nose. She switched on her lipsticky smile and turned it up to maximum. "Anyway, dahling boy, the only decision you've got to make is what you'd like a grateful woman to give you? Money? Slaves? Chunky gold necklaces…?"

Suprema certainly had a soupy voice. Ruff's face was getting all sweaty just listening to her and it suddenly got worse.

"…girlfriends?"

His knees went wobbly and his tongue fell out of his mouth. He backed away desperately looking for something that was the exact opposite of *girlfriends*.

Luckily she was waiting for him with her long wrinkly legs sticking out from under her tiny cutesy dress.

"Hiya, Mr Judge!" smiled the eighty-seven-year-old baby. She skipped around him and Ruff had to swallow hard to keep his guts down. "You must be ever so clever if you can decide who's the best."

"True," said Ruff. "But you've been a great help."

"Have I?" she gushed, rolling her eyes in excitement.

"Oh yes. At least you've made it easy to decide who's the worst."

In the box on the prizes table, the pink sheep and the green giraffe were having an urgent discussion.

"I wish we could let Googoobah win," said Tangal, stretching her long knitted neck to see what was happening.

"We can't risk it," said Tangor. "Just suppose he got kidnapped, and then something happened to him. We'd be baby-minding for eternity!"

"You're right," said Tangal. "We must make it impossible for Ruff to pick him. Maybe we could give Googoobah a pig's head? Or octopus arms?"

"That's dodgy," said Tangor. "It's hard to turn morphisms back. And if Googoobah grew up as a freak,

Wedge wouldn't like it."

Tangal stretched her green giraffe neck just a bit further when

PURRiPP!

"Ow!" she cursed. The stitching had given way and a lot of thick brown horse hairs had burst out. "Oh no, I'm losing my stuffing."

The little pink sheep hopped with excitement. "That's given me an idea! Suppose we gave him something freaky now, but when he grew up it'd look normal?"

"I'm sure that'd be OK," said Tangal. "But what?"

"You'll see!"

Meanwhile the crowd had been waiting anxiously for Ruff to make his mind up. As usual, Robbin had been carrying Raymond's bags on his back when a sudden giggle came from one of them.

"What's up?" asked Robbin.

"Something's tickling my ear!" said Raymond's voice.

"Like what?"

"Like a little brush. Hee hee, there it is again."

Robbin swung the bags to the ground. "Maybe one of your eyebrows is rubbing up against it. I'll have a look."

"No!" said Raymond. "It's not the ear in the bag, it's my other one. The one Gubbs is sucking. Hee hee!"

Robbin squinted his eyes and peered up to the stage. Sure enough, Googoobah was being very good and quiet and sucking on Raymond's ear, but... "Hey, Molly," said Robbin. "Look at Googoobah. Can you see something different?"

"Er, ooh, I'm not sure," said Molly. "Hey, you lot, what do you make of Gubbs?"

On the stage Divina looked down to see her family all staring at Googoobah intently. Could there be something wrong? Trying not to panic, she checked. His little cardigan was spotless, he was wearing both booties, his few hairs were tidy, his little cardigan was perfectly laced up, his nose wasn't snotty, there wasn't a hint of dandruff on his great big sticky-out handlebar moustache and most importantly his little cardigan looked divine. Well, if something really was bothering them, it can't have been all that important.

Ruff had had a good look at the other two babies and was now walking towards her. Divina began to feel quite relaxed. It didn't matter if she was Ruff's mother or not, she knew she had the bonniest baby, and there's absolutely no way anybody could ever find anything wrong with his hair, cardigan, nose, booties … GREAT BIG STICKY-OUT HANDLEBAR MOUSTACHE?

Divina blinked to make it go away. Blink. Blink blink. Blinkety-blinka blink BLINK blink. She tried to flick it off with her finger. No? Never mind, surely she could just wipe it away. She did a little spit on the very end of her sleeve and tried to rub it off. No, it wasn't quite going to go yet. "Has anyone got a razor?" she asked the crowd, before realizing that it wasn't the cleverest thing to say while holding a baby. Now *everybody* was staring. Just a bit more spit, a bit more rubbing, then a bit more spit…

By the time Ruff got across to Divina, her sleeve was absolutely soaking. It hadn't worked. Ruff was staring at Googoobah's upper lip in amazement. The little chap himself was happily sucking away on Raymond's ear, then he stretched his hand out, pinched the end of the moustache in his fingers and gave it a proud twiddle.

goo goo bah

"Honestly, Mum!" he said. "You know I've got to be fair about this. How can he be the bonniest baby with that brush growing out of his face?"

Divina clutched Googoobah tight to her chest. "Now you just listen here," she hissed. "I am your mummy. And down there are your daddy and your brothers." Ruff saw Urgum and the boys were scowling at him and had their nastiest weapons out. "While you were gone they've had nobody to hate, but if you let Suprema beat me, they'll have an awful lot of catching up to do."

Before Ruff had time to argue the dizzalid came and took him over to the prize table. "When you're ready," she said. "First prize is the golden nappy, second prize is silver. Present the silver nappy first."

Divina and Suprema were staring at him desperately, while behind them the old baby was doing happy little skips and pirouettes. Oh boy, what was he supposed to do?

In the box the giraffe's head was lolling down by its feet. "What's happening?" said Tangal. "I can't see. We sent so much hair over to Googoobah's top lip that my neck's too empty to hold my head up."

"It's not good," said the little pink sheep, peering over the edge of the box. "Divina just told Ruff that if Googoobah doesn't win, the others are going to marmalize him."

"What? Googoobah CAN'T win with that moustache! Ruff would look very stupid. Surely he'd rather be marmalized than look stupid. He must have some pride."

"This is Ruff we're talking about."

"Oh. Oh dear."

"Here he goes!" said Tangor, wagging his little pink woolly tail. "He's made his mind up. Oh no, he's taking the silver nappy over to Suprema!"

"NOOOO! That means Googoobah is going to win."

"Wait, he's walked past. He's given silver to his mum. Googoobah's not going to win, so he's safe!"

"Hooray for Ruff!" they both cheered.

But nobody else was cheering for Ruff. The crowd booed, Divina hissed and Urgum and the boys were barging their way on to the stage for a quiet word with him. The only person who wasn't completely hating Ruff was Suprema, who was radiant with joy. Already she'd turned to Divina. "See?" she said. "See? See? I told you I could raise a child better than you."

Ruff knew he had to move fast. Before Urgum could get his hands on him, he dashed back to the prize box to grab the golden nappy.

"Ladies and gentlemen," he announced loudly. "May I present the winner." Ruff ran over to Suprema, who reached her hand out expectantly. He shook it and said, "Hard luck, missus, but well tried." Then he pushed past her, grabbed the skipping baby and thrust the golden nappy into her bony fingers.

YAR-A-HOOO!

The whole of Dream Valley erupted in delight.

The old baby skipped around, waving her golden nappy over her head and blowing kisses to everyone. Her happiness was so infectious that Urgum and the boys skipped around and blew kisses too. Officals swarmed over the stage to organize the winners' parade, and in the confusion, a small nursemaid with spiky hair hurried over

to the old baby to dress her in the golden nappy.

"I'll manage, dear," said the old baby. "I've been doing my own nappies for years."

The nursemaid's grey face looked confused, but when she saw Divina beaming with joy and Googoobah sucking on the silver nappy, she went to help there instead. There were already some people from *Modern Savage* magazine offering congratulations and a reporter pushing for an interview, so before she knew it, Divina had passed Googoobah over while Glamora gave her a nice cool cherry water to sip and everyone round her made a fuss. The only person not celebrating was Suprema. She was still locked in position with her eyes glazed over and her hand held out waiting to take the prize. Eventually she was carted away by her giggling slaves while the clowns blew their tooty trumpets. It was wonderful.

Molly was helping Ruff clean the rest of the gooey slime off his clothes. "I can't believe you've made everybody so happy," said Molly. "That was just so brilliant."

"Oh yeah? It just so happens that I'm brilliant all the time," said Ruff snootily. "Can you believe that I passed right through a giant bird and came out the same as I went in?"

"Maybe that's not so hard," said Molly. "It just depends on what you're made of in the first place."

DUNCH CRACK
BUNCH
KRUNK

A deafening noise came from the garden stairs leading down from the entrance.

"URGUM!" shouted Mungoid. He'd seen his old friend skipping round the stage blowing kisses and ploughed through the crowd towards him. "URGUM, URGUM," he shouted again, mainly to fill time until he got there.

Urgum had no idea what Mungoid wanted, but he was pretty sure it wasn't a kiss. "Robbin, brace yourself to stop him!" he cried, and along with his biggest son, he leapt off the stage and together they held their hands out as the great Ungoid came hurtling towards them.

BOOOOF!

Too heavy to stop quickly, Mungoid barged into their hands, pushing Urgum and Robbin back quite a long way before they all came to a halt and fell over with Mungoid lying on top of them.

"URGUM!" shouted Mungoid, right in Urgum's face, just in case he hadn't noticed him.

"What?" asked Urgum, pushing Mungoid off.

"Googoobah mustn't win the competition!"

"He didn't win."

"Thank goodness," said Mungoid rolling over and sitting up. "Because the winner's going to be kidnapped."

"You're kidding! Why?"

Mungoid took a few deep breaths to steady himself. "I overheard some troggyls. They'd decided that the winner had to be the prince and they're planning to get him."

Urgum burst out laughing. "They must have got wind of Suprema's plan. If it wasn't for Ruff, then yes, the winner would have been the prince!"

"So you mean the prince didn't win?"

"Relax, old mate! Look, that's the winner up there. Does she look like a prince to you?"

Mungoid snorted in disbelief when he saw the old baby prancing around in her gold nappy. "Ho ho! They won't be kidnapping her, that's a fact."

Ho ho ho, laughed everybody.

"Mind you," said Mungoid. "That means they'll probably go for whoever came second."

"Pah, all these silly numbers," scoffed Urgum. "I don't

care so long as Gubbs is safe."

"DAD!" said Molly. "Gubbs came second."

"Eh?" said Urgum, holding up his fingers. "I thought it went one, two, four, three ... where does second come into it?"

But Mungoid and Molly were already dragging Urgum on to the stage. Divina was wide-eyed and shaking her head in disbelief. "I had him, and then this woman was asking questions, then the nursemaid took him to get changed…"

"The prize box has gone," said Molly. "She must have smuggled him away in there."

"What did this nursemaid look like?" asked Urgum.

"I don't know, I didn't really see her!" wailed Divina.

"Grey-faced?" said Mungoid. "Short, spiky hair?"

"There was somebody like that," said Glamora.

"She was a troggyl," said Mungoid. "But where did they go?"

"DAD! Over here, this way!" Molly was at the back of the stage peering off the edge. There was a tiny thin strand of blue wool caught on one of the supports which ran down to the ground and disappeared off into the distance. "It's from Googoobah's cardigan. The nursemaid must have climbed down here and run off."

"Follow that wool!" shouted Urgum, and he leapt off the stage, immediately followed by Mungoid, Divina, his seven savage sons and Molly.

OOFCRUNCH
ARGH
OWYOWEEGERROFF

Once they were all back on their feet, they ran along through the trees and undergrowth following the trail of wool. The sides of the valley got steeper and narrower until they found themselves at a dead end looking into a low archway cut into the rock.

"They must be in this cave," said Urgum breathlessly. "Right, here's the plan. I charge in, you all follow. That's the plan. Now, do you want me to go over the plan again or have you got it?"

"Got it," they all said.

"It's a bit dark in there," said Ruinn. "What happens if we lose you?"

"Use your super-special barbarian senses," said Urgum, closing his eyes and taking a deep, meaningful sniff. "Feel the ancient magic guiding you along."

"What does that mean?"

"What he means…" said Molly, "… is that you have to follow the smell from his trousers."

"Get ready," said Urgum. "We go in fast, we go in hard." He took a few steps back from the dark entrance so he could make a run-up.

"Urgum, I recognize this place," said Mungoid. "I've got a bad feeling about this."

"This is no time for your feelings!" shouted Urgum.

"Listen to me!" said Mungoid, stepping in Urgum's way. But Urgum wasn't having any of it. He turned to the boys and screamed their blood-curdling battle cry:

"ARE WE SCARED?
NO!
DO WE CARE?
NO!
WE'RE COMPLETELY
MENTAL!"

Mungoid was still blocking the entrance. "Honest, Urgum, there's something you should know…"

"The only thing I know is that there's a little boy in there who needs me, and if you stand in my way, then I'm going in over your dead body," screamed Urgum.

Mungoid shrugged his shoulders and stepped aside.

"CHARGE!" cried Urgum. He ran into the darkness, but before anyone could follow him there was an almighty

KRUNCH

"YOWGARGH!" cried Urgum, staggering back out again clutching his head.

YOWGARGH...
YOWGARGH...YOWGARGH...

Long booming echoes came out of the archway.

"As I was saying," said Mungoid. "Watch out for the low roof."

"Stupid cave," cursed Urgum. "And why is it still making that noise?"

…yowgargh … yowgargh…

"That's the other thing. It's not a cave." They all looked at Mungoid uneasily. "Troggyls live together in a big colony that moves round underground. This is the perfect place for them and a very bad place for us."

"Why, what's down there?" somebody asked, but nobody looked round to see who it was because they were all too busy staring at Mungoid.

"The Uninteresting Tunnels," he said.

"Ah, yes, you refer of course to that spectacularly dull network of underground passageways lying deep below the jagged rocks and shifting sands of the Lost Desert which stretches from beyond the Forgotten Crater right over to the Upside Down Lake." The seventh son was rather proud of his knowledge, but unfortunately for him, everybody was so busy staring at Mungoid that nobody realized he'd been talking.

"I hate to say this, but right now Googoobah could be anywhere," said Mungoid.

Urgum put his big arm around Divina's shoulder. He could feel her whole body shaking with anger, fear and misery. Her hair had fallen loose from the silver comb that usually held it pinned up. He ran his fingers through it. "I don't like you being upset," he said. "So stop it."

"What'll happen to him?" asked Divina quietly.

"He'll be fine," said Urgum. "They think he's royal so he's far too valuable alive for anything to happen to him. All we've got to do is go and get him back."

Urgum made it sound so easy, but none of them were fooled. The only one brave enough to say what everybody was thinking was Mungoid.

"Urgum, those tunnels go on for ever. You'll need a whole army to get him out," said Mungoid.

To everybody's surprise, Urgum chuckled, then he gave Divina an extra squeeze and wiped a tear off her nose with his finger.

"That's all right then," he said. "Because I've got one."

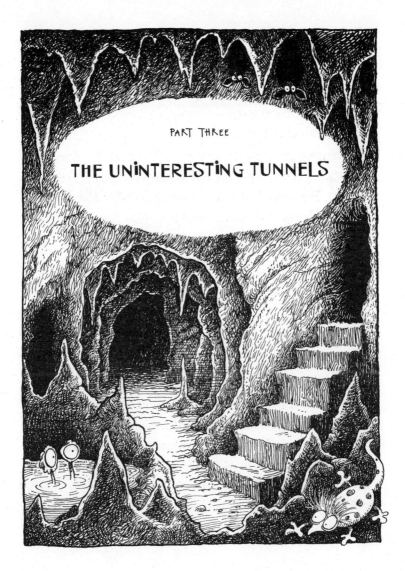

PART THREE

THE UNINTERESTING TUNNELS

Hats and Lampshades

The sun had set and Dream Valley was completely dark apart from the odd torch flickering away in the gloom. The crowds for the baby show had all departed a long time ago, leaving the stage bare and the gardens empty. The only noise came from the officials' tent, where Urgum was standing on a table in front of a huge gathering of big, brutish and strangely dressed savages. Earlier on, the knitter boys had been packing up their stall at the craft market when Ruinn had arrived to say Urgum was offering them a gruesome evening of extreme danger. The word immediately spread round, and when Ruinn returned, he didn't only bring Leg

Warmers, Tank Top and Fluffy Scarf, but also the cake-stall guys, the pottery dads, the frilly-lampshade brigade, the ornamental candle dippers, the hair-braiding mob, the lacy-curtain crew, the squashed-fruit barmen and the embroidered-shoulder-bag gang. Urgum wasn't surprised. After a hard day of mixing kumquat and celery juice or rubbing herbal cream into strangers' toe cracks, any decent savage needs to unwind a bit.

"This is the plan," Urgum was saying. "We go in, kill the troggyls and get Googoobah. Have you got that?"

"GO, KILL, GET," chanted the savages approvingly. It was a clever, detailed and well-thought-out plan.

"How will you see?" came a little voice from the back.

"Eh?" said Urgum.

"I said, how will you see?" The mass of heavy shoulders parted so that the little stalls manager could step forward in his hat six sizes too big.

"Hunjah, what are you doing here?" said Urgum irritably. "This is a tough fighting force but you're the patheticest barbarian that ever lived!"

"I'm here to do my bit," said Hunjah, sounding hurt.

There was a general muttering about whether Hunjah should be tossed out of the tent door even if he was the stalls manager, but Molly had climbed on to the table by Urgum.

"Hunjah's got a point," she said. "It'll be pitch-black down in the tunnels, and you can't all rely on the smell of my dad's trousers to guide you."

There was a sigh of relief. Nobody had wanted to rely on the smell from Urgum's trousers.

"You'd better think of something," warned Hunjah. "There's one tunnel that's so dark, nobody has ever found it. It's even got a nickname."

"What?" asked Tank Top by accident.

"It's called The Darkest Tunnel."

"So how do you know it's there if nobody's found it?" asked Leg Warmers.

"Because it'd be a bit silly giving it a name if it wasn't there, wouldn't it?"

"HUNJAH!" shouted Urgum. "Please, just shut up."

Two of the savages were rummaging in the boxes they

had brought from the craft market. "Maybe these will help?" said the ornamental candle dippers, handing round some long perfumed candles.

"Perfect," said Urgum. "Right, lads, let's go over the plan once more."

"GO. KILL. GET."

"What about a uniform?"

"Hunjah, SHUT UP."

"No, really," said the little barbarian. "There's going to be a big mix of savages down there."

YAWN, went everybody, but this time Divina spoke up.

"He's right. We don't want you killing each other by accident."

Fluffy Scarf rather sheepishly opened a bag he'd been carrying. "What if we all wear these?" he asked, pulling out some yellow knitted bobble hats.

"Super!" said Divina.

Soon most of the savages were wearing yellow bobble hats, but there weren't quite enough to go round. The ones without were having a good snigger at the others but, before it exploded into a fight, Divina silenced them all with a killer glare.

"Has anybody got anything else we can use for hats?" she asked.

The frilly-lampshade brigade opened up a box they'd

brought, and finally all the volunteers were hatted. There was some giggling and pushing but Urgum had his axe out. "This is serious, so anybody who laughs gets a slice of THIS!"

GULP! went everybody.

"Right! Now get ready to hit them hard and hit them fast," said Urgum, waving his candle and adjusting his frilly lampshade. "Because when they see us coming, they're going to be very scared."

The air outside the tunnel entrance was thick with the smell of perfumed candles. Divina had organized it so that Urgum and the boys would lead the way in, then the rest would follow, splitting up into their teams to go off searching. That just left Hunjah as the odd one out, sitting by himself on a rock with a candle sticking out of the top of his hat.

"You wait out here for us, Molly," said Divina.

"Hang on!" said Urgum to Divina. "Who's this 'us'? You're not coming in, are you?"

"I might recognize the nursemaid who took Googoobah," said Divina. "But it's far too horrible, dark and smelly in there for Molly."

"That's unfair!" said Molly. "Why isn't it too horrible, dark and smelly for you, then?"

"When you've shared a bed with your father for as long as I have, you're ready for anything."

"I'm not sitting out here alone!" sulked Molly.

"You won't be alone," said Divina. "There's Hunjah. You can be on his team."

"Oh, MUM!"

It was no use. Divina had already gone to join Urgum, which hadn't been Urgum's idea at all.

"Come on, dear, say it," said Divina, giving him a nudge.

"Say what?" said Urgum blankly.

"Oh for goodness' sake, I'll do it." Divina turned to face the others and took a deep breath.

"YARGHHH!"

she cried, making all the frilly bits on Urgum's lampshade quiver.

"YARGHHH!" shouted everybody, and off they all charged into the blackness of the tunnel.

DONK DUNK CLONK ZONKATY BUNK

"Watch out for the low roof," came Mungoid's voice from the darkness.

Molly went over to sit by Hunjah and be sulky. "I hate being the one that's left out looking stupid," she said.

"Don't worry about it," said Hunjah. "They're the ones that are going to look stupid."

"Why?"

"They'll never find the baby. Those tunnels are a real mess, they'll just be running round in circles."

"How do you know so much about them?" asked Molly.

"I used to be the tunnel guide," said Hunjah. "Nice little job too. I had a little tour all worked out with a running commentary."

"So why did you give it up?"

"Nobody ever came to look. They're not very interesting, you see."

Molly looked at Hunjah who was just sitting there letting the wax from the candle drip on to his hat. She knew he'd done some strange and sad jobs, but the tour guide for the Uninteresting Tunnels? No wonder he was known as the patheticest barbarian that ever lived. Hunjah got to his feet and took a few steps towards the tunnel entrance. "Come on, then. Teams are supposed to stick together."

"Mum says I've got to stay out here."

"Oh, that's a pity," said Hunjah, sitting down again. "Why?"

"I know where they'll have taken the baby, of course."

The Grilling

Urgum had promised everyone a gruesome evening of extreme danger, and they weren't disappointed. The tunnels branched off in all directions: sideways, upwards, backwards. Some led to other tunnels, some to larger caverns, and some to dead ends. The cake-stall guys were the first to have an encounter with a vicious band of wandering sentry troggyls who charged out of the gloom with their flint knives flashing in the candlelight. The cake guys managed to beat the first few off, but when a back-up team arrived they turned and ran, emptying a sackload of cream and strawberry horns behind them.

SKLURK SLODGE SPLADD!

The sentries skidded helplessly on the rocky tunnel floor, cracking their heads on the walls. The cake guys returned, and after dealing out a few extra **BIFFS**, the grey-faced sentries threw down their knives and gave in. The noise had brought Robbin up to find them. "Nicely done," he said. "We've found a central cavern to use for grilling them, so bring them down."

Elsewhere the soft-fruit barmen had had a similar success squirting pepper lemons into the enemies' eyes and leaping on them while they couldn't see. In the next tunnel, a marauding troggyl strike force ran straight into a fine net that had been strung across by the lacy-curtain crew. Most of them had got completely tangled, but one managed to double back, only to be walloped in the face by a novelty cow-shaped whistling milk jug.

MOO-DONK!

By this time a crack squad of elite guard troggyls had been

alerted. They were hardened fighters trained to deal with swords, daggers, arrows, spears, maces and clubs. Unfortunately for them, they had no idea what to do when the pottery dads fired off a lethal shower of butter dishes and drove them straight into an awesome barrage of rock-filled embroidered shoulder bags.

KRUMP DUMPH CLOMP! BLAPP

Eventually a whole selection of beaten and bashed troggyls had been herded into the middle of the grilling cavern. The elite guards were in grubby armour while the others wore their thick leather tunics. Ruff, Robbin, Raymond, Ruinn, Rekk and Rakk were guarding all the narrow exits. Curiously, there was also one huge exit, but that was being guarded by the seventh son that nobody ever noticed. It would have been the easiest way out apart from the fact that the seventh son was so ignorable, nobody had noticed there was an exit right next to him either.

Urgum and Mungoid had already begun to grill the spiky-haired savages, but it wasn't going well.

"Where is the baby?" Urgum demanded, raising his axe over their heads in a scary way. "You will tell me!"

"Eh?"

"Baby? Where?"

"Eh?"

The grey faces looked completely bewildered, so Urgum lowered his axe, folded his arms and rocked them as if holding a baby. "Baby, see? Well?" While Urgum was doing sign language, Mungoid took over doing the scary stuff. Slowly he opened his mouth further and further and further. His eyes glared, his great Ungoid teeth glinted, his tongue lolled down past his chin. The troggyls looked worried, but still couldn't get the message. What did these two huge savages with lampshades on their heads want them to do?

"Come ON!" threatened Urgum. "My mate hasn't had his tea and you look TASTY. So think about it. Where's the BABY?"

Urgum rocked his arms some more and Mungoid joined in. The troggyls glanced at each other, and then it dawned on them. They all folded their arms and started rocking them too.

"NO!" shouted Urgum, getting more desperate. "This isn't some sort of dance! LOOK at me." He screwed up his face and stuck his thumb in his mouth. "Wah wah wah!" Just to make things clearer, Mungoid scooped Urgum up in his arms and rocked him.

"Who's a liddle boodiful baby boy, then?" said Mungoid, leaning his head down and rubbing his nose on Urgum's.

"I want my bottle," yowked Urgum. "And I've filled my nappy. WAH!"

The craft-market workers were all standing around the edge of the cavern looking on in dumb shock. They weren't afraid of the dark or fighting or blood or nasty weapons, but watching those two was really unnerving. Divina was standing among them with her yellow bobble hat neatly pinned on top of her hair. She was suspicious of the way that one of the smaller troggyls hadn't been joining in, and then she saw him raise his hand to cover his mouth. Too slow! Divina had only caught the merest glimmer of a smile, but that was enough – he knew something. In a fury she stormed across and yanked him out in front of the others. Mungoid immediately put Urgum down, then the two savage friends stood back and straightened each other's lampshades. Divina stared at her victim and spoke very slowly in her coldest voice. *"You may not understand my words, but you do know what I want. You will now tell me. Where is the baby?"*

One older spiky-haired savage standing at the end of the row made the mistake of saying "eh?" In an instant Divina whipped round towards him. Her eyes narrowed and her left eyebrow locked into the "kill kill kill" position. The old troggyl clutched his face in terror and stumbled backwards into Ruinn, who drew his gutting knife and leered his ghastliest leer. The troggyl made no effort to get away. Whatever Ruinn might do to him couldn't be as awful as facing that eyebrow.

Slowly Divina ran her eyes back along the row of troggyls and the cavern echoed with the clenching of teeth and knocking of knees. The troggyl in front of her was already trying to tell her something.

"What is he saying?" asked Urgum.

"I can't make it out," said Mungoid. "Wood? A hole? Another hole? It's something about some wood in a hole with a hole in it."

"Did anyone see any wood in a hole with a hole in it?" asked Urgum.

The sons and the craft-market workers all shook their heads.

"*Where?*" Divina demanded, but before the talkative troggyl could answer, the head of the elite guards leapt forward and smashed him to the floor, where he lay unmoving. It wouldn't matter what Divina's eyebrow did now, he wasn't going to tell her any more.

Ruff, Rekk and Rakk charged over to grab the guard and drag him in front of Urgum. The grey face hissed and spat as the axeman bared his sharpened teeth and raised his axe ready to swipe off the guard's head.

"Urgum, don't do it!" said Divina. "He was only doing his job."

"And I'm doing mine," scowled Urgum.

The guard tried to struggle free but then Divina caught hold of Urgum's arm. "Stop – look!" A piece of parchment was poking out from the guard's armour. Divina pulled it out and was just about to unfold it when the guard tugged his hand free from Ruff. He snatched the parchment back and stuffed it in his mouth and chewed frantically.

"Well, go on then, quick before he swallows it!" said Divina.

Urgum brought his axe down.

KLOTCH!

The troggyl's head shot across the cavern and Ruinn leapt up and caught it. He ran around in delight, tossing it up and down in front of the other troggyls, who all whimpered in fear. "I've always wanted to do that!" he smirked.

"What's so special about that parchment thing?" asked Urgum.

"We better find out," said Divina. "Get it out of his mouth."

Ruinn tried to force the jaws apart but couldn't. "The teeth are clamped shut," he said helplessly.

"Oh don't be so pathetic," said Divina grabbing the head off him. She stuck her fingers up inside the severed neck and groped around, making the dead

troggyl's eyeballs swivel and bulge.

"URGHHH!" said everybody, clapping their hands over their faces, but then watching through their fingers anyway. Urgum felt Mungoid give him a nudge. They were both thinking the same thing. Divina might have been brought up as a softhand, but she could be more savage than any of them.

Everybody was very relieved when Divina finally found the parchment and pulled it out. She wiped it clean on the spiky hair, then chucked the head away and unfolded it.

"Look, Urgum!" she said triumphantly. It seemed to be a picture of a very big and complicated cobweb with a few blobs stuck on it. "It's a map of the tunnels, but I can't read the troggyl writing."

"Oh great," moaned Urgum. "So you can't tell what anything is, then?"

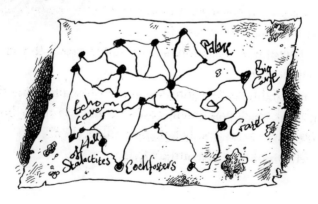

"Mum can't, but I can," said Ruff, who had come to look over her shoulder. "That's the Forgotten Crater, that one's the palace, there's the Unsightly Hills of Napp…"

"How do you know?" said Urgum.

"I saw them all from the sky," said Ruff. "That's exactly how they're laid out. The only one I'm not sure about is that purple bit."

"That's just a bit of troggyl brain," said Divina, flicking it off. "But look, if the tunnels go under the palace, that must be how the troggyls were getting in! They must have secret trapdoors in the floor."

"Who cares about the palace?" said Urgum impatiently. "Where are we?"

Divina looked around the cavern, then stuck her finger on the map. "We're exactly here," she grinned. "This cavern has seven tunnels, and this is the only place with seven lines coming from it."

There was an impressed mumble from the craft-market army.

"All right," said Urgum, who didn't like admitting that a bit of soggy parchment could be any use to anybody. "So where's the woody hole hole thing, then?"

"I don't know," admitted Divina.

"So in other words, it's useless," said Urgum.

The impressed mumble turned into a depressed grumble, but just then, one of the bags that Robbin was carrying started to twitch excitedly. Raymond had something to announce!

Wood in a Hole
with a Hole in it

At the same time as Urgum was busy in the grilling cavern, Molly had been following the candle on Hunjah's hat. She reckoned she must have walked halfway under the Lost Desert. Hunjah had led her along, round, up and down tunnels, tunnels and more and more tunnels, and he hadn't stopped talking the whole way.

"…You'll notice how in front of you this tunnel gets a bit narrower, but once you've got past it, something strange happens." They squeezed through. "Now if you turn back, you'll see the narrow section is now behind you…"

"Hunjah!" said Molly in exasperation.

"...and if you look upwards, you'll notice how the ceiling of this tunnel not only reaches right across, but also runs the entire length from one end to another..."

"Of course it does, it's a tunnel!"

"I was just doing a bit of my guided tour for you," said Hunjah, sounding a bit hurt. "It isn't easy trying to make the Uninteresting Tunnels interesting, you know."

But then Molly did see something interesting. In the darkness ahead, there was a tiny spot of light hovering in mid-air. She pushed past Hunjah and ran towards it.

"It's a little door with a keyhole!" whispered Molly excitedly.

"Aw, you guessed," sulked Hunjah. "I was saving that up for a surprise. It's one of the tour highlights. It's

known as the wood in the hole with a hole in it."

"There's a light on the other side."

"I thought there would be," said Hunjah. "It's the mess room, the only place down here that can be locked. Perfect for holding the baby."

Molly bent over and peered through the keyhole. A flaming torch on the wall showed three troggyls standing around a table. Two were wearing rough leather armour but the third was wearing a nursemaid's dress – and when she stepped aside, there on the table was the prize box!

"Hunjah, you've done it!" hissed Molly. "He's in here, but how do we get in?"

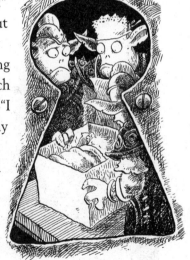

"Easy," said Hunjah, pulling out his ridiculously huge bunch of keys and selecting one. "I always keep keys, it's one of my hobbies."

"Don't open it yet!" said Molly. "He's not alone. We need some way of getting past them."

"Let me have a look," said

Hunjah. He put his eye to the keyhole and tried to understand what he was seeing. A pink knitted sheep's head had risen over the edge of the box and seemed to be looking directly at him. And then it winked.

"Fancy that! A pink sheep just winked at me," said Hunjah. "And now there's a green giraffe with a floppy neck getting bigger and bigger and bigger…"

"Hunjah!" snapped Molly irritatedly. "You can make up all the silly stories you like. You're still never going to make these tunnels interesting."

"They've both jumped out of the box now and they're attacking the troggyls."

"Forget it, Hunjah," said Molly. "These tunnels are the boringest thing ever."

WHAM!

Hunjah jerked his head back as something collided with the other side of the door.

THUMPBASHCLOMP

"What's going on?" said Molly.

"I told you, the pink sheep and the green giraffe are attacking the troggyls."

"Hunjah, if this is some sort of joke…"

"See for yourself."

Molly had a look but the noise had stopped and the room now seemed empty. She stood back to let Hunjah unlock the door and open it. There was no sign of any pink sheep or green giraffes, but the three troggyls were sprawled out on the floor unconscious. Molly rushed over and looked inside the box.

goo goo bah!

"Gubbs!" exclaimed Molly, picking the baby up and giving him a big hug. His spiky moustache tickled her neck, but she didn't care. All that mattered was that he was alive, well and smiling. "Come on, we're getting you out of here!"

goo goo

The baby was pointing back in the box. Molly saw the little pink woolly sheep and the giraffe with the lolling neck.

"Sorry, Gubbs," she said. "We can't carry everything. But we better take Raymond's ear."

Just then some troggyl grunts came echoing out of the darkness of the tunnel. "There's more coming!" said Molly. "Is there another way out?"

"No," said Hunjah. "This room is a dead end."

"Oh no!" said Molly. "I'll never be able to get Gubbs out past them."

"Oh yes you will," said Hunjah, passing her his hat. "Put this on and hide behind the door. I'll distract them, and that should give you a chance to sneak away – good luck!"

Molly dashed behind the open door and peered through the crack by the hinge.

goo goo bah!

"Shhh!" said Molly, slipping Raymond's ear into Googoobah's mouth. "We have to trust Hunjah."

As soon as the troggyls came into sight and saw the door open, they barged in and stumbled over their three friends sprawled out on the floor. Molly held her breath as the nursemaid got her senses back and explained what had happened. Obviously the others had trouble believing her, but they looked all around the room and back out into the tunnel. It was just as they were coming over to check behind the door that a cry came from the prizes box.

"Wah wah!"

They went back over to the box and looked inside.

"Wah wah WAH!"

While they were distracted, Molly quietly nipped out from behind the door and dashed out down the tunnel. One of the troggyls reached into the box but when he lifted out the crying bundle, the blanket wrapped around it slipped away.

"Wah wah and just for luck, one more WAH!"

The troggyl dropped Hunjah's head in disgust, but before they could all go charging out, Hunjah's headless body had crept out from under the table, felt its way around the wall and kicked the door shut.

BLAM!

It didn't take the troggyls long to shove the groping torso aside and wrench the door open again, but Hunjah had given Molly enough time to get out of sight.

Molly kept running and running, dodging and ducking through different holes and cracks, hoping that she'd bump into somebody wearing a lampshade or a bobble hat, but all around her was eerie silence. Pausing for breath, she took off Hunjah's hat and saw the candle had gone out. That was odd – she could actually *see* it! What was going on? Most of the underground had been dank and cold, but the rocks around her were warm, and above her the ceiling was even glowing with a dim red light. If only there was some way of telling Urgum and the others where she was...

goo goo buh! Buh-huh! Buh-huh!

Googoobah was starting to cry. She couldn't blame him. It must be terrifying for the little boy, but he had to stay quiet for all their sakes in case the troggyls heard him.

"Give Raymond's ear another chew," she said, but then she saw he'd dropped it on the floor. Molly picked it up and was just about to pass it back when she realized what to do.

"Raymond?" she whispered into the ear. "Raymond, can you hear me? Listen carefully..."

And that was when, back in the grilling cavern, the bags

on Robbin's back had suddenly twitched with excitement.

"Careful!" said Robbin. "I nearly dropped you."

"Shhh!" said Raymond's voice. "I can hear Molly and she's got Googoobah."

"MOLLY'S GOT GOOGOOBAH!" shouted Robbin, and everybody cheered massively. The sound echoed off and away down all the tunnels under the Lost Desert. Far far away, Molly heard the noise. She couldn't be sure which direction it had come from, but at least she felt that her message had been heard.

"I'm in a strange place," said Molly to the ear. "The walls are hot and the roof is glowing red."

Raymond passed the message on.

"I don't believe it," said Urgum. "She must be right underneath the Forgotten Crater! Thank goodness we've got that map. Tell Molly we're coming to get her."

"OK," said Raymond, but then he remembered he couldn't talk through his ears. Well, it would have been a bit strange if he could, wouldn't it?

Left alone in the mess room, Hunjah had found his head, put it back on his shoulders and swivelled it round so that it was facing forward. It was a long time since he'd been in the Uninteresting Tunnels and he'd really enjoyed trying out his guided tour. If only there was somebody to tell about the crack in the rock where he used to keep his biscuits. Or the funny mark on the floor that looked a bit like a banana. Hunjah sighed, then remembered the prize box. He took out the little pink sheep and the green giraffe and stood them on the table.

"Ladies and gentlemen," he said, looking upwards. "If you care to cast your eyes to the highest part of the roof, you'll notice how it happens to be the bit furtherest away from the floor…"

But when he looked down, his audience had gone. Oh

well, he'd started his tour, it seemed a shame to give up now.

"...you may be disappointed that there's only one door in here, but the extraordinary thing is that it gives you complete access to the whole of the rest of the universe..."

The Crumbling Cavern

The tunnel Molly was in was too hot for comfort, so she made her way along to an opening in the end. She stepped through and found herself standing on a narrow ledge that overlooked an enormous underground cavern. Patches of the walls were glowing with a deep-red colour, giving enough light to show that, although the floor was flat, it was littered with huge boulders. There was creak and a rumble from up above.

Weee-KRAKK!

A huge rock fell from the roof and crashed down to join the others. The noise caught Molly by surprise and made her step backwards. Ow! The wall at the back of the ledge was glowing so hot it had almost burnt her. Molly tried to spot a way down, but when she looked over the side, all she could see beyond her feet was smoky blackness. Beneath the ledge was a chasm which ran all the way along. Even if she wasn't carrying Googoobah, Molly knew she'd have no chance of jumping it.

She was just about to go back into the tunnel when she heard distant grunting noises coming out. There were troggyls down there somewhere, and she couldn't risk meeting them, so all she could do was clutch Googoobah to her chest and make her way as far as she could along the ledge. And then – did she imagine it?

"You walk in front with the candle. I'll follow with the axe."

"Why? I'm the best fighter! YOU go in front."

"Stop pushing and gimme that axe!"

"I'll give it to you in your HEAD soon."

Molly grinned with relief. It was Rekk and Rakk's voices coming from some unseen opening in the shadows on the far side of the cavern. She did a quiet whistle to try and attract their attention, but not too loudly, in case the troggyls heard.

"Mum definitely said I could have the axe."

"But you got the light shade. I only got a bobble hat."

"Tough!"

"I'll give you tough…"

"Rekk! Rakk!" she called softly. There was a silence.

"Hey, that sounded like Molly."

"MOLLY!"

There was a crunch and a clump and then she saw a

flicker of yellow light in the gloom. The twins stumbled into view, clutching a candle.

"Over here!" Molly waved her hand.

"Thank goodness we found you," said Rekk as they ran towards her.

"Yeah," said Rakk. "Molly, tell him to give me that axe!"

"But that's unfair. Mum said—"

"Shut up, you two!" said Molly. "Where are the others?"

"We'll get them!" said Rakk.

The twins went back the way they came.

"DAD!" they yelled. "DAAAAAAD!"

There was creak from the roof as another boulder came loose.

Weee-KAJAKK!

Soon the tunnel openings on the far side were echoing with voices. Yellow bobble-hatted savages started appearing and the whole place shimmered with the light of scented candles. Eventually a large frilly light shade walked across to the chasm and Urgum peered out from underneath.

"Goo goo bah!" said Googoobah, waving excitedly at Urgum.

"Hello, mate," said Urgum, waving back. "Thanks for looking after my little Molly. Now, then, we better see about getting you home." He looked down over the edge at the swirling fumes. "Nasty! Never mind, we'll think of something."

Footsteps were coming from the tunnel hole up on the ledge. Molly hugged Googoobah close to her and then suddenly the troggyl nursemaid's head popped out. At first the troggyl was so surprised to see Urgum, she just stood there and stared until she realized that the chasm would stop him getting any closer. Pulling out her flint hammer, she made her way along the ledge towards Molly.

Back on the cavern floor, Mungoid grabbed an embroidered shoulder bag and shoved a meaty-sized rock inside it. "Keep back," he warned the others as he swung it round and round his great head. He let go.

WHeee-cLUMP!

The bag flew across the chasm and blatted the nursemaid hard in the stomach. With an agonized cry she doubled up and backed into the red-hot wall where her bottom caught fire. Screaming, she leapt forward and plummeted off the edge down into the darkness below. There was a loud **HISS** and a plume of nursemaidish smoke drifted up.

"HO HO HO!" everybody laughed massively.

"Serves her right," grinned Mungoid.

FSSSS-tHYUP!

An arrow with an orange feather thudded into Mungoid's light shade.

"THERE YOU ARE!" came a very unpleased voice from the darkness at the back of the cavern.

Everybody turned to see Grizelda aiming a second arrow at Mungoid. Her flame-coloured hair seemed on fire in the eerie red glow from the hot rocks. "And exactly *WHAT* serves *WHO* right?"

"What's Grizelda doing here?" gasped Urgum.

"Goodbye, Urgum," said Mungoid. "I'm about to be dead."

"Not yet," said Urgum. "She hasn't come all this way down here to kill you without making a big speech first."

Sure enough, Grizelda took a big breath, then let Mungoid have it. "So you thought you'd get me to meet you in the Parad-Ice Cream Parlour and then suddenly remember something more important and dash off, leaving me looking like a lemon? Thought you could hide underground and have a big laugh with your mates about it?"

"Sorry," mumbled Mungoid.

"Too late for that. You are going to die very very slowly. This arrow is tipped with tortoise venom, the slowest-acting poison in the Lost Desert. It could take you years to die. Ha!"

"Fire away," said Mungoid, facing Grizelda full on and raising his hands in the air. "I deserve it."

"Hang on!" said Urgum going to stand between them.

"Mungoid came to warn us about the troggyls. Without him we'd never have found the baby."

"Troggyls?" said Grizelda. "Baby?"

"He's stuck up there with Molly," said Urgum, pointing.

Grizelda's bow started to waver uncertainly. "Oh, I see. Now you're trying to make me look foolish and selfish, are you?"

"No, not at all," said Mungoid. "What does saving a baby's life matter compared to waiting for you to finish your pudding? Stand aside, Urgum, and let her shoot me now."

"I can't shoot you," said Grizelda. "I feel rotten."

"Sorry," said Mungoid again.

"Look, you can shoot him later if you want, but right now I need to get on to that ledge," said Urgum. "If we tie a rope to an arrow, could you fire it up there?"

Grizelda nodded.

"Brilliant!" said Urgum. "So who's got a rope?"

Everybody checked through their things, but although they were fully equipped with fruit, leg warmers, cream buns, shoulder bags, lacy curtains, sugar bowls and candles, nobody had a rope. A peculiar growling noise came from Grizelda, then she snatched the yellow bobble hat from

Rekk's head and grabbed Ruinn's long gutting knife. Still growling, she picked out three of the craft-market savages and without a word, she led them into the blackness beyond the cavern. There was a burst of strange noises.

SKRIT SWIT SHWOK

Everybody waited and whispered. What was the flame-haired assassin doing with that knife?

"She's gone mad," said Rakk.

"Not as mad as Dad," said Rekk. "Fancy thinking he can walk across a rope."

"But he can," said Robbin. "When he was a kid he used to walk on a rope across the bear pit. It was really dangerous because if you fell in, you had a gruesome fight to the death."

"But Dad was always fighting nasty animals in the bear pit," said Rakk.

"Yes, but he never fell in," said Robbin. "No, he always had to jump in. He loves gruesome fights to the death."

"There wouldn't be any gruesome fighting down there," said Ruinn, staring at the chasm. "One slip and he's serious toast."

"I'm not scared," said Urgum. "Dying gloriously and stupidly is what barbarians do. My gods will welcome me as a hero and feed me divine nectar for ever."

"That'll be a fat lot of good to Molly and Gubbs," said Robbin.

"Oh," said Urgum. "I never thought about that."

Grizelda returned with the yellow bobble hat pulled down tightly over her head. The three savages followed her, one of them with a shiny bundle of something piled in his hands. Without a word she climbed up on to the highest boulder and then peered over at the ledge, looking for a suitable weakness in the rock. She put an arrow to her bow, took aim and fired it straight across the chasm. Trailing behind it was a long, sleek, shimmering length of orange cord. The arrow sunk deep into the rock.

"Good shot!" said Urgum. He threw his axe aside, took the other end of the cord from the savage and quickly tied it to a stump of rock on the ground. "Where did you find the rope?"

"None of your business," snapped Grizelda. "Just get up there and get on with it."

Urgum put his foot on the cord to test it. "It's very thin," he said.

"Don't you worry," said one of Grizelda's helpers with hushed admiration. "You could bounce an elephant on the end of that."

"How do you know?" asked Urgum.

"We're the hair braiders. We know the best hair when we see it."

Mungoid looked up to see Grizelda sitting on top of the boulder with her knees drawn up in front of her face. Her hands were sadly stroking her bobble-hatted head. He wished he could think of the right thing to say to her.

Very carefully Urgum put one foot and then the other on to the cord. The lowest section was just above the ground and cut so sharply into his boots that he could feel it on the soles of his feet. Ahead of him the orange line stretched up towards the ledge where Molly and Googoobah were watching him. Keeping his eyes locked on them, he slowly started to make his way along the cord and out over the edge of the black chasm. Behind him the boys shouted stirring words of encouragement.

"Go on, Dad!" shouted Ruinn encouragingly. "Just pretend you're crossing the old bear pit."

"Yeah, Dad," shouted Robbin. "Just pretend there's a pack of hungry bears down there."

"Yeah, or that six-headed bull you keep bragging about," shouted Ruinn.

"Or that lion-headed eagle," shouted Rekk.

"Or that crocodile-headed gorilla," shouted Rakk

"Or that duck-headed duck," shouted Robbin.

Urgum was halfway across when below him the chasm rumbled and belched. A thick cloud of yellow sulphur smoke wafted up into his face making his eyes water and his head swim. Step by painful step he crept onward, his lungs starting to burn and the cord cutting through his feet. Even the encouragement coming from the

boys had gone a bit off-subject. "Which one was the duck-headed duck?" shouted Ruinn.

"You know," shouted Robbin. "That one that looked just like a duck."

"I remember it," shouted Rakk.

"Yeah," shouted Rekk. "In the end it turned out to be a duck."

"A bit like the sheep-headed sheep," shouted Robbin.

"Yeah, but more duckish," shouted Ruinn.

Urgum's knees ached, his hands sweated, his head swum. He tried to clear his eyes from the stinging mist by looking upwards, but that made the whole cavern seem to swirl around him. He only had a few more steps to go, but his weight on the cord made the very last bit much steeper. His feet couldn't quite keep a grip, the ledge was just out of reach, then suddenly he slipped and fell forward. With a last desperate lunge he reached out and his hands grabbed the firm rock. He heaved and dragged himself upwards and then finally managed to turn and sit with his legs dangling over the edge.

goo goo bah bah goo!

Urgum rubbed his eyes and looked to see Molly and the excited baby beside him.

"And goo goo bah bah goo to you too, my little chum," said Urgum, stroking the little cheek with his finger.

"Well done, Dad!" said Molly. "So what's the plan?"

"The plan is that I lead you through the tunnels waving my axe so that anything or anyone in the way gets minced. Clever, eh?"

"Er, not bad," said Molly. "Apart from one thing."

"What?"

"You forgot your axe."

And there it was, still lying back down on the cavern floor.

"Oh bother," said Urgum. He hopped back on to the rope, slid down to the other end, grabbed his axe and skipped back up to Molly and Googoobah on the ledge.

"Dad!" exclaimed Molly. "I thought crossing the chasm was a slow, dangerous and painful thing to do?"

"It can be," agreed Urgum. "But the fun wears off after the first time, so I thought we better get a move on."

But then a squad of the elite guard troggyls burst out on to the ledge armed with their nasty flint hammers and daggers. Mungoid and the others slung some more boulders at them, but they were coming out too fast, ducking and crawling towards Urgum and Molly. Urgum tried to hack them back, but on the narrow ledge against the baking rock wall, there was no room to swing his axe properly.

"Get right back, Molly!" cried Urgum. "I've got to do something else."

He raised his great axe over his head and then smashed it down into the glowing wall.

TRANK!

A small dark crack appeared in the red rock.

"Dad!" shouted Molly. "What are you doing? That slab of rock is all that separates us from the boiling insides of the Lost Crater!"

"Yes, that's what I thought too," said Urgum, and he smashed his axe into it again and again.

KRUNK!
BRANK!
ZANK!

The troggyls' eyes opened wide in panic as suddenly

the crack split wide open. A white-hot jet of molten rock spewed out over the ledge, taking the nearest guards with it. Soon the whole wall was crumbling away as a deluge of fire gushed over the chasm and across the floor of the cavern. Urgum and Molly backed right to the far end of the ledge, shielding their eyes from the heat with their arms.

Down in the main part of the cavern, everyone scarpered to the far end and scrambled up to safety in the higher tunnels. Soon the floor was awash with white bubbling magma, leaving just one solitary figure

stranded on a boulder.

"Grizelda!" cried Mungoid from the back of the cavern.

Grizelda raised her head from her arms and looked round, but it was too late. She was on a little island surrounded by liquid fire, there was no way off.

"Mungoid!" she screamed, reaching out towards him. "Mungoid!"

Then the ceiling started to creak and groan and the first few small boulders fell into the magma, splashing up white-hot blobs of liquid rock. The boys watched Mungoid anxiously as he climbed back down again.

"Don't do this at home, kids," he grinned then he plunged his foot right into the pool of flames.

"YOWWWWWWW!"

His cry echoed around the cave. He dragged his foot out with the liquid rock sticking to it like a burning boot. He waved his leg around and soon the magma had cooled enough to set solid.

"YOWWWWWWW!"

he cried as he repeated the operation with his other foot. Once he had both feet encased in solid-rock wellies, he slowly waded out through the flames towards Grizelda, who clambered into his outstretched arms and clung to his neck. The great Ungoid turned and waded back just as the main part of the cavern roof collapsed behind him.

Half a Rhino

The sky was red with the early-morning sun as a sorry procession made its way across the Lost Desert towards Golgarth Cragg. Mungoid was sitting sideways on his ox with his bandaged feet dangling down like two fat pillows. Riding beside him, Grizelda was slumped wearily on her horse, still wearing her yellow bobble hat. The sons rode alongside Divina, their horses all plodding along without enthusiasm.

"We shouldn't have come home without Dad," said Robbin. "We should have waited to see if he got Molly and Googoobah out."

"What's the point?" asked Ruinn. "We all saw the

cavern collapse."

"At least he died a glorious and gory death," said Rekk.

"It's what he always wanted," said Rakk.

"Lucky old Dad!" said Ruinn. "So which glorious and gory death do you think he got in the end?"

"Crushed by boulders," said Rekk.

"Nah, he fell down the chasm more like," said Rakk.

"I bet he was dissolved in the river of fire," said Ruinn. "Which one do you think, Mum?"

"Be careful, lads," said Robbin. "Can't you see Mum's upset?"

"Sorry, Mum," said Ruinn. "We were forgetting Molly and Gubbs had a glorious and gory death too."

"Oh yeah!" said the twins. "Sorry."

"So what do you think happened to them?" asked Ruinn. "Crushed, fell or dissolved? Or perhaps it was one of each?

But Divina wasn't listening to this jolly conversation. She wasn't even thinking. She couldn't think. She just rode on.

Meanwhile, somewhere deep down below in the blackness, a milligob was coming to the end of a long, luxurious and completely undisturbed feast. This milligob had been extremely lucky because ages ago it had been caught by a freak rainstorm. Normally that would have meant bye-bye milligob because a milligob was nothing more than a flabby white stomach covered in tiny mouths. But this one had been washed underground and carried along until it had come to rest against a burnt animal carcass. Immediately the tiny mouths had all opened up to reveal thousands of needle-like teeth and it had set about greedily chewing its way inside. Many days and nights had passed, but the milligob didn't care, just so long as it could gorge itself without having to share with anyone or anything else.

Apart from mouths, milligobs only have tiny legs so that they can roll over when the mouths nearest the food get tired. They certainly don't have ears, because that would be a waste of space that they could have used for more mouths.

However, if this lucky milligob had got ears, it wouldn't have been too pleased at the sounds

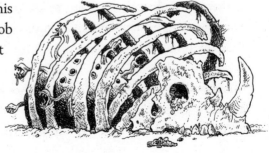

that were echoing towards it.

"Keep up, Dad," said a girl's voice.

"But we've tried all these tunnels," moaned a very grumpy man.

"No, we haven't. I've been marking the ones we've done with chalk. There's still this one left."

"If only that cavern hadn't collapsed, we could have got Gubbs safely home and into bed by now."

"Stop moaning!" said Molly. "It blocked off all the troggyls and opened up that hole at the end of the ledge for us. All we have to do is keep making our way uphill, we're bound to come out somewhere."

A glimmer of yellow light fell across the milligob and a clatter of footsteps ran towards it. "Oh that's totally vommo!" Molly exclaimed delightedly. "You've got to come and see this, Dad."

More heavy footsteps followed as Urgum eventually caught up. He had the sleeping baby cradled in one great hairy arm and his axe over his shoulder.

"Oh yippee," he said. "It's only a milligob sucking on half a rhino skeleton."

"Yeah, but Dad, that's not all. Look at the torch flame!"

"What about it?"

"It's flickering, you great ninny! There must be a draught coming from somewhere."

"Where?"

"THERE!" shrieked Molly, holding the torch high and looking straight upwards. "Woo-hoo!"

goo goo bah!

"Careful! You've woken him up."

"Don't care. WOO-HOO!"

goo goo goo bah bah goo!

"What's so brilliant about up there?"

"Gubbs knows, don't you, Gubbs?"

"He knows WHAT?"

"Oh, Dad! Don't you realize where we are?"

Up above, the sorry procession had reached Smiley Alley. They were nearly home and Divina was bracing herself. She knew she had to be strong for the sake of the others.

"Nearly there, Mum," said Robbin. "But how are we going to get in? Olk won't let us through without Gubbs."

"It'll be all right," said Divina. She had no idea why she'd said it, but it was easier than saying, "Urgum is dead, Molly is dead, Googoobah is dead, Grizelda has lost her hair and Mungoid's feet are burnt to the bone." Just to make things worse, the two Golgarth vultures, Djinta and Percy were circling overhead. That was a bad sign. "It'll be all right," she said again, trying to convince herself.

Divina put her shoulders back, ready to face the

worst, and sniffed back a tear. Then she sniffed again. And again. What was that smell? It was very faint but yes – there it was! Her whole face wrinkled. It was disgusting, horrible, revolting … and the most gorgeous smell she had ever smelt in her life.

"It'll be ALL RIGHT!" she shouted and gave her horse a whacking great SLAP on the bottom. The astonished beast shot forward and charged down towards Olk.

"How do you know, Mum?" cried the boys, trying to keep up.

"Can't you smell them?" cried Divina joyfully. "Can't you SMELL them?"

"Smell what?" shouted the boys.

"Your dad's whiffy trousers!"

When they got to Olk, Divina pulled up her horse impatiently.

"Password!" boomed the great guardian. The foul blade twitched on his shoulder.

Divina leant over so she could look round Olk through into the basin. "URGUM!" she screamed. "URGUM! URGUM!"

Olk thought about it. "Urgum" was the wrong password, but he wasn't sure if he was supposed to slice Divina in two or not, as it was her who usually gave him the orders. His eyes flickered in their sockets at the selection of people arriving in front of him. Where was the little password-speaking person? He wasn't with them. They must have left him out in the Lost Desert somewhere. Well, Olk wasn't having that!

"PASSWORD."

"URGUM!" shouted Divina again, and then sure enough, the great big whiffy-trousered savage stepped out of their cave along with Molly. Cradled in his arm was the smiling, waving baby.

goo goo bah!

"Uh?" said Olk. He tried to understand what had happened. He knew that the last time he had seen his little friend was on his way out because Olk had done a little *bye bye* wave. And ever since then Olk had been waiting patiently to do a little *hello again* wave, yet somehow his little friend was already back inside the Cragg. Olk had been looking forward to doing his *hello again* wave, and nothing was supposed to get past Olk. The great guardian of Golgarth had somehow failed in his task. His head hung in shame, and the blade slipped from his grasp to the ground, slicing an extremely unfortunate frog in half on the way.

KARR-A-DANG! **ReBBiTT**-URGHH.

Poor Olk. At some future time he'd be told how Urgum and Molly had brought Googoobah up from the Uninteresting Tunnels by climbing up the hole underneath the kitchen fireplace, but it would have to wait. It was time for fire, food, fizzy drinks and fun.

Jealous?

Divina was having a morning in the cave catching up with the news in *Modern Savage* magazine. Now that the kidnap threat was over, Laplace Palace was arranging a grand ceremony to mark the return of the prince. There was also an exclusive picture of the "Prince's Mystery Mum", who had been secretly looking after the royal infant and she was saying, "*Dahling!* Whatever made you think it could be *me?*" No wonder Suprema was looking so smug. Obviously when the prince was to be taken back to the palace, she'd be going along too.

Divina wasn't wasn't *wasn't* going to be jealous. Oh

no. Of course, there had been a time in her life when she'd have given anything to be invited to the palace, but that was when she'd just been a shallow softhand spending Daddy's money. All that had mattered to her then was who she knew and where she was seen. Her life had  changed completely since she'd been married to Urgum, especially after the adventures in the Uninteresting Tunnels! All that mattered now was to know that little Googoobah was safely playing outside under the watchful eye of dear old Urgum.

Outside in the rock basin, dear old Urgum was indeed looking after little Googoobah as only a true barbarian can.

"His walking's really come on, hasn't it?" he shouted proudly.

"Yes, he never falls over now," Mungoid shouted back from the opposite side of the bear pit.

There was a rope stretched between them and Googoobah was toddling along it, while down below a few starving leopards paced round impatiently. Urgum had his arms held out to catch the little chap as he stumbled off the end of the rope on to the firm ground.

"Goo goo bah!" said Googoobah, and he gave the end of his moustache a proud twiddle.

"Yes indeed, goo goo bah," said Urgum. "You're getting to be quite the young man with your walking and your moustache!"

"He still doesn't say much, though," said Mungoid, limping round to join them.

"He'll get his first word or two soon," said Urgum. "How're the feet?"

"Not so bad," said Mungoid. "I've just got a few more bits of dried lava stuck between my toes to chip out."

GOYY-ANGGGGG!

Lizards scuttled under rocks, ostriches buried their heads in the sand and all the horses' teeth rattled as the deafening sound echoed around Golgarth Basin.

"It's the door chime!" cried Divina as she hurried out of the cave over to the crack in the cragg wall.

"I wish she wouldn't call it that," said Urgum. "It's Olk whacking a giant gong with his elephant-stunning mallet."

Divina came back clutching a gold-edged sheet of gold with gold writing on it. Although it looked very posh, it was murder to read, but that wasn't going to stop Divina. As she slowly made the words out she almost rose off the ground in excitement. Finally she looked up.

"Urgie!" she said breathlessly. "We are going to the palace."

"Eh?"

"You, me and our youngest child are invited. I bet

they're giving you a medal for wiping out those awful troggyls!"

"Pah. I don't need a silly medal…"

"URGUM, WE ARE GOING!" Divina was already picturing the look on Suprema's face when she realized she wouldn't be the only one getting a bit of attention.

"If this is just some trick to make me change my trousers…"

"You can wear your trousers *and* your frilly lamp shade for all I care, but, URGUM, WE ARE GOING."

A Completely Unexpected Twist

When Urgum and Divina reached the palace they were ushered through to the grand antechamber. The invitation had included their youngest child, but as they couldn't decide whether that should have been Molly or Googoobah, they'd brought both. There were masses of people milling about and even before they got inside, they could hear the sound of tooty trumpets. Sure enough, there was the army of nannies, clowns and cooks, and in the middle of everything was Suprema on her sedan sofa, which was being carried by six strong slaves. She was holding a little bundle at arm's length.

"Well, of course you're expecting us!" she was saying crossly to the Grand Thake, who was a tall stuffy-looking man in the green and gold official robes of the palace. "How can you celebrate the return of the prince without the prince?"

The Thake obviously wasn't going to let them get any further, so the slaves lowered the sedan sofa to the ground in front of him. "I regret, madam, that madam is making a mistake, unless this means anything to madam?" He held out his open hand to show a small flat object resting on his palm.

Suprema glanced down briefly. "What's this? Some sort of silly party game?"

"I thought as much," said

the Thake smugly. "Madam hasn't a clue, has she, madam?"

"Of course I've got a clue. It's a nasty little coin that's been cut in half. Now do go away."

Divina was standing back in the doorway carrying Googoobah. "Half a coin?" she wondered and instinctively reached for the little pouch that hung round her neck. It was where she kept the kisskey that she'd found in Googoobah's bag.

A small woman in an immaculate white robe hurried over. "You are the people from Golgarth, aren't you?" she said earnestly. "Oh thank you so much for coming. I am Jannilah, Mistress of the Royal Bedchamber."

"How do you do," said Divina. "I am Divina, this is my daughter, Molly, and this is…"

"…Urgum the Axeman," said Jannilah, her eyes beaming. "The fiercest savage the Lost Desert has ever known. I'm honoured to meet you, sir!"

Oooh! Urgum liked being called sir. He felt so posh that he accidentally did a little curtsy. Jannilah was smiling at Googoobah, who smiled back and gave his moustache a twiddle. "What a marvellous disguise," she said.

"DIVINA!" Suprema's voice cut through the room. "How dare you come crashing in here with that …

freak?" She got off her sedan sofa and stormed through the crush carrying her own baby.

"We were invited," said Divina simply. "Were you?"

"Invited?" Suprema gulped. "Oh, well, maybe *you* need to be invited, but not me. Looking after the prince makes me almost one of the family."

By now the Grand Thake had made his way over to them, and Jannilah asked him to produce the little half coin again. Suprema sniffed scornfully. "Why do you keep waving that stupid thing around?"

Urgum didn't like coins and money at the best of times, and seeing the half coin had stirred up a really worrying thought. "Suprema's right, dear," he said, trying to lead Divina away. "It's just a stupid thing, so let's stop bothering these people and take Googoobah home."

"No, Urgie," said Divina. She took the kisskey from her pouch and held it out towards the official. When the two half coins were put together they fitted exactly. "He is home."

"Gosh! Wow! You mean *Gubbs* is the *prince?*" Urgum slapped his leg in amazement and shook his head. "What a completely unexpected twist. If this was all to be written in a story book one day, nobody would *ever* suspect that."

A dreadful wail came up from Suprema.

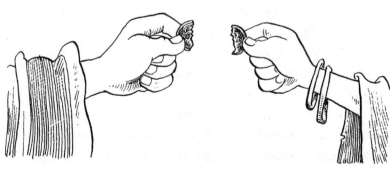

"Nooooooooo!" she said. "It can't be!" She rounded on Jannilah. "You delivered this kid to me yourself. You said the prince was in danger of kidnap, so could I look after the child?"

"Yes I did," said Jannilah. "But I never said that child was the prince."

"Of course he's the prince!" said Suprema. "I should know, I've bonded with him! When I think of all the times I changed his little nappies…"

All the nannies immediately hissed crossly. Divina raised her eyebrow to interrogation setting. "You? Changed his nappies? How many times?"

"Hundreds," declared Suprema. The nannies shook their heads. "Well, dozens, then." The nannies shook their heads. "Quite a few times!" The nannies still shook their heads. "Well, all right, I did it once and it was absolutely the most disgusting thing ever." But the nannies were still shaking their heads. Suprema turned on them. "You liars. I DID change a nappy, you all saw me."

"That wasn't a nappy," said one of the nannies. "That was a bib."

"What's that got to do with anything?" said Suprema. "All that matters is that this is the prince and nobody can tell me different."

"I can," said Jannilah. "Because that's my own baby daughter."

"DAUGHTER? You mean he's a GIRL?"

There was a cackle of laughter as all the nannies nodded and smirked, and at that point the baby woke up and did a tiny little yowk. Suprema automatically passed her away to the nearest person, who happened to be Jannilah.

"My baby!" cooed Jannilah as the little girl gurgled in her arms.

"She's been a little treasure," beamed one of the nannies.

"We'll really miss her," said another.

"Do you think she remembers me?" asked Jannilah anxiously.

"Mmmm … mmumm … mum … MUM!" said the baby, and Jannilah burst into tears.

"That's silly," whispered Urgum. "Fancy crying just because somebody says mum."

"Yeah, well it needn't worry you," replied Molly. "Nobody will ever call you mum, Mr Big Fat Smelly Trousers."

Both Suprema and Divina were staring wide-eyed waiting for an explanation. Hugging the baby to her chest, Jannilah explained. "Even though the palace is guarded, somehow prowlers were getting into the private rooms."

"Tunnels and trapdoors," said Molly.

"Yes, but we didn't know that then, so we had to find somewhere else safe for the prince. I knew the best protection he could get would be from the savages of Golgarth, but I wasn't sure how you'd react to having a softhand prince thrust on you. You might even have left him out on Sacrifice Rock."

"What? Gosh! Me? Never!" said Urgum. "Pah, as if I'd ever—"

"Shut up, Urgie," said Divina.

"Me? Shut up? What a good idea," said Urgum.

Jannilah continued. "So I dressed him as a savage and, sure enough, you adopted him as one of your own."

"So why did you give me your kid?" demanded Suprema.

"After a few days I realized that we also needed a decoy. And you did the most wonderful job," smiled Jannilah. "As long as you were parading around, nobody would go looking for the prince up at Golgarth. The palace owes you its deepest thanks."

"Oh really?" snapped Suprema. She pulled a copy of

Modern Savage from the sedan sofa and angrily poked the front page. "Look at this!"

"Prince's Mystery Mum!" said Molly. "Nice picture of you."

"What will people say when they find out it's all lies?"

The nannies all started sniggering, but Molly cut them short. "People won't say anything because nobody is going to tell them."

"WHAT?"

Molly spoke to Jannilah. "Suppose you ever need to

hide the prince again, we'd always have him back, wouldn't we, Dad?"

"Yes!"

"And as long as nobody ever knows he was with us, it'll be easy," said Molly. "It just requires a huge favour from Suprema."

"What?"

"You must promise us that for the rest of your life you go round bragging to everybody that you are the prince's mystery mum"

Jannilah nodded. "The palace would never deny it."

"You could do exclusive interviews," said Molly. "You could make up stories like 'My Royal Nappy Changing Hell' and 'Sleepless Nights Ruined My Hair Style',"

Suprema's eyes were wide in excitement.

"Do it, dear!" said Divina. "You could give them 'Shopping Tips for Palace Mothers'."

"Yeah," said Urgum. "Or how about 'Playing With the Prince Made me into an Ugly and Selfish Old Witch'. OWW!"

Molly had given Urgum a hard kick, but luckily Suprema was already away in a celebrity dream world. She couldn't believe it! She was going to be allowed to brag about how she'd helped the palace as much as she liked, and she'd never EVER have to change a revolting nappy-bib-whatever-it-was-thing again!

"But now," said Jannilah to Divina, "if you'd be kind enough to hand over the prince, the princess awaits him."

The Grand Thake reached forward, but Urgum snatched Googoobah from Divina's arms and held him tight. "Oh no you don't!" he said.

"But, Dad, you've got to," said Molly.

"Urgie, it's for the best," said Divina.

Urgum rounded on them. "Remember at the baby gala, you handed him over to somebody you didn't know, and look what happened. I don't know who these people are, so I'm sure as not handing my little mate over to them."

"These are palace people," said Divina. "You have to trust them."

"Oh yeah?" said Urgum. "But what about the mum? Who knows what she'll say when she sees Gubbs has got a great big sticky-out moustache? I'm not letting him go until I know he's going to be absolutely all right. So I'm going to pass him over to the princess myself."

"But, Dad, you can't!" said Molly. "Nobody ever sees the princess. She's so beautiful you'll go blind."

Urgum hugged the little boy to his great chest. A deep growl came from the back of his throat. "I'd rather risk my eyesight than risk Googoobah," he said.

Goodbye For Ever.
Whatever. Big Deal.

Down a black stone corridor, through a black banging door, up a few black steps, round a black corner, along a black-carpeted black passageway, more black doors, black steps, black corners…

Eventually Urgum gave up trying to work out where he was, he just walked on carrying Googoobah with the Thake leading him by the arm. Before he'd left the antechamber, Jannilah had passed Urgum a thick blindfold, which naturally Urgum had refused to put on, but Divina and Molly had refused to let him refuse, so on it had been put.

Urgum was just starting to think they'd never get there, when the Thake suddenly came to a halt and said, "We're here." Urgum heard a rustle of cloth as he put on his own blindfold. While he waited, he reached his hand out ahead of him and his fingers met with a solid wooden door. Urgum found himself hugging on to Googoobah harder and harder. It had only just dawned on him that when the time came to walk back, his little warm bundle would be gone. No more goo goo bahs and little friendly waves. Urgum had to remind himself that he was a hardened savage, the last of the true barbarians, and so he didn't care. Not one bit. It would just be goodbye for ever, whatever, big deal.

"Is sir ready?" said the Thake.

"Get on with it," said Urgum slightly rudely.

The Thake knocked, then pushed the door open. "Your majesty?"

"Please, do come in."

Urgum thought it was a rather nice girlish voice. But there again, if she was supposed to be so beautiful, she'd hardly sound like Mungoid sticking his feet in a lake of molten lava, would she? Once inside, Urgum found the room was quite warm, it had a thick carpet underfoot and smelt of apple pie.

"You've brought me a visitor!" The princess sounded pleasantly surprised.

"Your majesty, this is Urgum the Axeman," said the Grand Thake.

"You mean the fiercest savage the Lost Desert has ever known?" said the princess excitedly. "Has he come

to slaughter us all and toss our bones to the milligobs?"

"Sorry, not today," said Urgum. "I'm having one of my Urgum the Nursemaid days."

Beside him the Thake hissed. "Her majesty was asking me, not sir. Sir will *not* speak unless she speaks to sir first."

The princess laughed. "Are you serious? I'm sure Urgum the Axeman says whatever he likes to whoever he likes whenever he likes."

Already Urgum liked this princess a lot. He could feel Googoobah twisting round in his arms to look at her.

"Oh!" gasped the princess. "My baby! But you didn't need to bring him all the way down here yourself. You could have left him with the Thake."

"I wanted to be sure that you wanted him," said Urgum. He could feel Googoobah proudly twiddling his moustache. "After all, he has changed a bit."

"Yes, he has," sighed the princess happily. "They grow up so fast, don't they? He's really got the family look about him now."

"He has?" gasped Urgum.

"So, please, may I take him?"

"No!" Urgum said with a sniff. "I'm not handing him over to somebody I can't see."

"Sir is being obstinate," said the Thake. "Doesn't sir know that her majesty's beauty will strike sir blind?"

"That's better than sir passing the baby over to the wrong person," said Urgum, and then he found himself doing an even bigger sniff.

"Urgum," said the princess. "You are prepared to risk your eyes for the sake of my son?"

"That's why I'm here," said Urgum.

"So be it," said the princess. "But first the Thake must wait outside."

"But I can't leave your majesty alone with the savage! Think of the risk."

"He is risking more than I am," said the princess. "And besides, we won't be alone, I have my son to protect me."

"Goo goo bah," agreed the son.

Urgum heard the Thake go, shutting the door behind

311

him. "Very well, Urgum the Axeman," said the princess. "If you are ready, then so am I."

Urgum gave Googoobah one more hug. He didn't know what was going to happen but it had to be worth it. He took a deep breath, braced himself then whisked off the blindfold. The throne was golden. The dress was golden. Her eyes were golden. Her hair was golden. But strangely enough, her long thick bushy beard was green.

"So..." said the princess nervously. "You've seen me."

"I have," said Urgum wondering quite what he was looking at. She wouldn't be as old as Divina, but she was a lot fatter and her skin was bone white. Obviously this poor girl never got daylight, never got exercise, in fact, she never got out at all. Urgum knew an unfortunate person when he saw one. And, most importantly, he could still see her. His eyes weren't being affected at all.

"You're the first person who has ever dared look at my face in years," said the princess. "You see, ever since this…" She fingered her beard as she struggled to think of the right words. "…my mother was very proud, but then shortly after I was born … well, she started this rumour about me being so beautiful…"

"Sometimes parents get it so wrong," said Urgum. "Like my father on his deathbed, the last thing he did was pull off his trousers. He passed them over and told me to wear them for ever in his memory."

The princess stuck her nose out towards Urgum, then wished she hadn't. "I believe you," she said, trying not to breathe. "But how could he be so cruel?"

"Family tradition," said Urgum. "His father had done it to him and his father before that…"

Behind the beard, the princess smiled, and Urgum couldn't help smiling back.

goo goo bah!

Urgum had almost forgotten he was carrying Googoobah. "Well, here he is," he sniffed, and then he did another sniff, followed by a sniffly-sniff. "At least I know he's going to the right person."

"You risked blindness to be sure?" asked the princess.

"He's a, *sniff*, grand little, *sniffle*, lad," said Urgum as he gently lowered Googoobah into the princess's lap. "He's, *sniffle*, worth it, *snifffff*."

Urgum watched Googoobah looking up into the princess's eyes. She ran a fond finger along his smart moustache, he reached up to stroke her soft cheek. Urgum's nose was starting to run. Funny, it wasn't that cold. He did one more massive sniff to get it sorted out properly and ended up making that noise that sounds like a fat duck being pulled inside out. Gosh, his nose was still really runny. It was so runny that even his eyes were starting to run too. OH NO – his eyes couldn't be running! That would be a bit like crying, but of course it wouldn't be crying because he was

URGUM
THE AXEMAN,

the last of the true barbarians! Barbarians didn't cry not

even when they were watching a little abandoned boy being handed back to his lovely mother who'd so obviously been missing him and…

OH NOT AGAIN

…his nose was dripping all down his vest and his eyes were getting all hot. Urgum bit his lip and concentrated on goodbye for ever, whatever, big deal.

"Does he talk?" asked the princess.

"No proper words," said Urgum. "Just goo goo bah." Then Urgum remembered that he might never hear his little friend say goo goo bah again. But so what? Come on, Urgum, it's only a little baby.

GET A GRIP

"Maybe one day he'll call me Mum," said the princess wistfully.

The little fingers reached out and entwined themselves in her beard. "Mmm…" said Googoobah.

"He's trying!" whispered the princess breathlessly. "Aww! Listen…"

"Mmm … ug … mmm"

"He's nearly saying it!" she gushed. "I can't believe it, his first proper word is going to be mum!"

Then a little hand broke free and pointed at Urgum.

"Uggum Daxman."

That's when, for the first time ever, the fiercest savage the Lost Desert had ever known cried his silly eyes out.

old Wet Eyes is Back

Molly and Divina were waiting in the antechamber when they heard footsteps coming down the dark corridor. The Thake was leading Urgum and, as he stumbled closer, they could see his blindfold was gone. One hand was clutching the Thake's arm, the other was clasped across his eyes. His shoulders shook, his footsteps faltered.

"The child has been delivered safely," said the Grand Thake. "And this is truly a great man."

"Urgie!" wailed Divina. She and Molly hurled themselves at him and led him to sit down. "Your eyes? What happened?"

"Dad, why did you take off the blindfold?" demanded Molly.

"I had to," gulped Urgum. He reached round, found Molly's head and stroked her hair. "I couldn't just pass him over."

"But what if you never see again?" said Divina.

"I don't know," said Urgum. "But I had to risk it."

Molly was peering very carefully at Urgum's face. There seemed to be an awful lot of water coming out from behind his fingers.

"Dad," said Molly suspiciously. "I hate to say this, but you look a bit like you've been crying."

"How DARE you?" Urgum cursed, jumped to his feet and staggered across the room. "*Me?* The fiercest savage that ever lived? *Crying?*"

"Then what's that wet stuff on your face?" asked Molly.

Urgum took several deep breaths, still refusing to uncover his eyes. "In case you'd forgotten, I have just come face to face with a woman so beautiful that she made my eyes melt! These aren't tears, this is special

MELTING EYE LIQUID."

"Urgie!" said Divina. "Does that mean … you can't see?"

"I don't know," said Urgum.

"There's only one way to find out," said Molly. "Take your hand away, Dad. Go on, do it!"

"No!" said Urgum.

"We have to know."

Molly grabbed the great wet fingers and slowly peeled them back from her father's face. His eyes were screwed up tight, but then very slowly, the muscles relaxed. One red-rimmed eye fluttered slightly then opened. It rolled around and saw Molly.

"Divina, it's you!" said Urgum.

"Stop it, Dad," said Molly, giving him a sharp poke in the stomach.

"Oof!" said Urgum. "Come here, Molly, I'll get you for that."

Divina watched amazed as Urgum chased the giggling Molly round and round the antechamber, under the table, up on to chairs and swinging off the torch brackets. "You can see, dear!" she gasped.

"Eh?" said Urgum, suddenly reaching out a hand and

groping towards her. "Is that your voice, my love? Oh yes, there you are! It's gradually getting clearer."

Divina held his ears and looked into his shiny green eyes and was overjoyed. But there was one thing she didn't quite understand.

"Why didn't the princess's beauty melt your eyes?"

"Oh, I can explain that," said Molly. Urgum shot her a warning look, but she continued. "It's obvious. Dad's so handsome, when he looked at the princess and she looked at him, they just cancelled each other out."

"Molly's right," said Urgum. "That's the honest truth."

"Of course it is," said Divina, moving her face closer and closer to his.

"Hey, remember where you are," said Molly, yanking Urgum back by the ear. "And you watch it, Mum, he'll make your eyes melt."

"That's nothing compared to what his trousers do to my nose," said Divina.

"Enough!" said Molly, dragging them to the door. "It's time to get you two home."

New Teeth, New Leader

Up in the Halls of Sirrus, Tangor and Tangal were disgusted.

"What did Urgum think he was doing?" wailed Tangor. "Our last true barbarian *crying?*"

"At least no one will ever know," said Tangal.

"But what if the princess tells everyone?" said Tangor.

"She won't dare," said Tangal. "Or Urgum could tell everyone about her beard."

"We should still punish him," said Tangor. "We could make his tongue swell up and explode or something."

"Why bother? He's got enough problems already!" chuckled Tangal. "Olk won't let them back into

Golgarth without the baby."

"Oh yes he will," came a voice from the doorway. They both spun round to see Daisybelle tottering in. Immediately the gods stuck their fingers in their ears and braced themselves for the screams. "Relax! This is just a social call. He's done very well, your believer, so I took the liberty of removing this from the sentry's brain." She held up a handful of chaos cobweb, then wiped her streaming nose on it. At least she wasn't dribbling quite so much as before and her cheeks didn't look so red. "So what do you think of my new teethies then?" she grinned. They saw several shiny little white stumps had finally broken through the gums.

"Very nice," said Tangal. "But where's Wedge?"

Daisybelle pointed outside. The stork was standing beside the blanket laid out on the cloud. Booty Bot had pulled Wedge's dummy from his mouth and was patiently poking him in the eye with it. Wedge in turn was whimpering for his mum.

"Wedge made the big mistake no baby can afford to make," sneered Daisybelle. "He got old. Things moved on, now I'm the boss. As for him – He Doesn't Matter."

Tangor and Tangal exchanged glances. They had no idea it was so merciless in the baby world. Daisybelle was eyeing them mischievously. Her pudgy hand grabbed a priceless antique vase from the bookcase and swung it around carelessly, just missing the wall and the table edge. Tangor and Tangal bit their lips, waiting for the *crash*, but then she carefully put it back on the bookcase. Very gently, she poked it with her finger until it was in the exact same spot where it had been before.

"Like I said, it's a social call. Of course, if you'd upset

us, then this little visit wouldn't be quite so pleasant. But as it is, we're very pleased with you. And if people make babies pleased, then we have a very special reward."

Tangor and Tangal stood transfixed as Daisybelle tottered towards them. Suddenly her fat arms reached forward. She grabbed Tangor by the ears and wrenched his face against hers. He didn't have time to shut his mouth tight before he felt a goofy dribbly kiss land on his lips, and the salty taste of runny snot land on his tongue. He was still feeling dazed by it when Tangal got the same treatment.

"So long then," said Daisybelle, turning to go. Obviously she was bored of walking, so she fell on to all fours. The last they saw of her was her big nappied bottom sticking out from under her little spotty dress as she crawled off to join the others on the blanket.

"What were we talking about before she turned up?" wondered Tangal.

"No idea," replied Tangor dreamily.

"Me neither."

Even ancient and mighty gods can't resist the magic of baby kisses when the worst things are all forgotten and the best things are yet to come.

A Party For One

"**G**OO GOO BAH!" shouted the craft-market army, proudly wearing their yellow bobble hats.

"Enter!" said Olk, and they all piled in to join the biggest party that Golgarth had ever seen. Rekk and Rakk had the vibes booming from their drum mountain while Ruinn set up the games. The other sons had got a huge bonfire blazing,

next to which was a rack of giant toasting forks. Alongside were heaps of dripping hippo tongues, stuffed eagles, red swan livers, ostrich legs, giraffe eyes, and (accidentally) a very small bowl of tossed salad. Molly and Divina were mixing up buckets of sauce, while Urgum and Mungoid were loading the punch juice fountain.

"It was nice of the palace to send us all this stuff," said Urgum.

"You deserve it," said Mungoid.

"We all deserve it." Urgum cracked open a barrel top and watched a few violent yellow bubbles fight their way out. "It's just a shame Grizelda isn't coming."

"Yeah," said Mungoid sadly. He stuck his finger in the squirming liquid, licked it and staggered backwards. "Ooyah!"

"So does it taste like a punch in the mouth?" asked Urgum.

"Absolutely." Once Mungoid's eyes had stopped rolling, he looked over at Grizelda's closed door.

"Go on, old friend, ask her again," said Urgum, filling a cup and passing it over. Mungoid grabbed it, guzzled it, groaned, grinned and gritted his teeth.

Grizelda was sitting and staring in her mirror at the yellow bobble hat on her head. Once again she ignored the tapping on the door, and even when Mungoid summoned up the courage to open it and peer inside, she didn't move.

"Please, Grizelda," he said. "Everybody wants you to come out."

"They just want to stare!" she snapped.

"No they don't," said Mungoid.

"Why not?" wept Grizelda, whipping off the hat. Her bald head was still covered in scars after her quick shave with Ruinn's gutting knife. "LOOK AT ME!"

Mungoid smiled. "Looking like that reminds us all of what you did. You've never looked so good."

"Oh? So now you're telling me you never liked my hair?"

Mungoid answered by reaching into his pocket and pulling out a tiny embroidered silk purse. It looked rather out of place in his big hand. "I got it from one of the craft-market lads," he explained sheepishly. Very delicately he slipped two fingers inside and then withdrew a long flame-coloured hair with a little tar blob on the end. "I've been keeping it safe. Do you want it back?"

Grizelda stared at it wide-eyed, then quickly nodded and faced the mirror again. Mungoid came and stood behind her, then laid the black blob on the top of her head. As he squashed it down with his finger, Grizelda drew a deep breath and held it.

"So … will you come to the party now?" asked Mungoid.

After a long time, Grizelda breathed out again. "OK," she said. "But not yet."

"Why not?"

"I've got to do my hair first, haven't I?" She picked up a brush and a comb. "So do you think I should wear it straight down? Or maybe set it over to the side?"

Mungoid gave it some thought. "Do you know what would really suit you? Just leave it looking wild."

When Grizelda stepped out of her doorway, just as she expected, everybody stared. She stood there glaring back defiantly with her chin high, shoulders back, hands on hips. Who was going to weaken first? Grizelda or the whole craft-market army?

It was just as she was about crumble and run back inside that the first loud whistle cut through the air. Then another and another and more and more. How dare they? Just because she was GORGEOUS it was no excuse for such gross disrespect. She strode down towards the bonfire, her eyes blazing in fury.

YAR-HOOOO!

The cheer lasted for ages and ages and a bit more ages. She was going to have to teach them some manners, oh yes indeed. Just as soon as she'd had a cup of punch and a stuffed eagle … and juggled a few snakes and had a bash on the twins' drum mountain and shown them all how to walk backwards across the bear pit.

Grizelda would have been a bit surprised if she'd known who had whistled first. Urgum had been quite surprised too, as Molly was sitting on his great knee when she'd done it. It had worked out just as Molly had hoped and now everyone was having the bestest time. There was just one more person who really deserved to be there, but Molly knew he'd be happier where he was, and she was right.

Somewhere deep down below the jagged rocks and shifting sands of the Lost Desert, a lone voice was drifting through the tunnels.

"…Meanwhile we have the curious 'tunnel of paradox', which has baffled experts for years because when you walk down it in one direction it curves to the left, but if you come walking back the other way, you'll find that it mysteriously curves to the right. As we pass through I'd like to draw your attention to the famous inverted stalactite, not to be confused with the conventional stalagmite, and that takes us into the passageway called 'The Greyest Tunnel', but if anyone wants to know how it got its curious name, I'll be glad to take questions at…

…the end."

KJARTAN POSKITT

is the bestselling author of the *Murderous Maths* series and many other books, most of which were illustrated by Philip Reeve. He was born and lives in York and has a wife, four daughters and about 1300 copies of the *Beano*.

PHILIP REEVE

worked in a bookshop for many years before breaking out and becoming an illustrator. He is also the award-winning author of the *Mortal Engines* quartet. Philip now lives on Dartmoor with his wife, Sarah, and their son Samuel.

LOOK OUT FOR

Kjartan Poskitt illustrated by **Philip Reeve**

A riotously funny saga packed with barbarians on horseback, bizarre creatures, interfering gods, man-eating plants and a very disgusting lavatory.

You'll laugh your head off!

LOOK OUT FOR

Kjartan Poskitt illustrated by **Philip Reeve**

Urgum's back! In an adventure packed with yet
MORE bizarre creatures, barbarians in bridal
gowns, evil villainous budgies … and some
LEGENDARY underwear.

You'll laugh till you fall over!

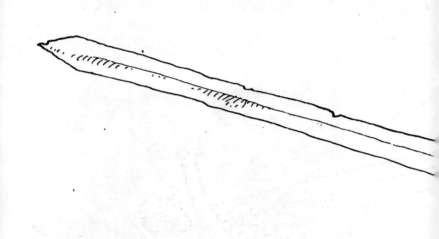